MURDERED
BY
COUNTRY MUSIC

A High Desert Cozy Mystery - Book 3

BY

DIANNE HARMAN

Published by: Dianne Harman
www.dianneharman.com

Interior, cover design and website by
Vivek Rajan Vivek

ISBN: 978-1532980077

CONTENTS

ACKNOWLEDGMENTS

As always, I really appreciate your taking the time to read my books, review them, and letting me know how much you like them. It's humbling, and I'm truly honored. Thank you, thank you, thank you!

This book is the latest one in the High Desert Cozy Mystery Series. There's a backstory on how I came to write it. I was having a little problem with my back and was seeing a physical therapist. One day while he was treating me several people around me began to talk about a music festival that was going to be held near Palm Springs. They were talking about mollies, Fireball whiskey, and how people came from all over the country to attend the festival. I became fascinated and started asking them questions. That's how Murdered by Country Music came into being. My sincere thanks to Chad Beauchamp and all the rest of the staff at Fitness Solutions. Without that conversation this book never would have been written.

I would be very remiss if I didn't thank the two people who are an integral part of why my books have become so popular. First there is Vivek, who patiently formats my books for both print and digital, as well as designing fabulous book covers. I sent him an email with a couple of sentences of what the book was about and that not only did I not have a working title for it, I didn't have a clue what the cover should look like. Later that afternoon I received an email from him with his proposal for the cover. It was perfect. How he interprets what I need when I don't even know what I want is a mystery to me! The second person I want to thank is my husband, Tom. He's very careful to make sure that my books are as error free as possible, particularly as to time and characters. He's even been known to forego a golf game for my books! Thanks to both of you.

And as I usually do, I want to thank my boxer dog, Kelly, (named after Kelly of Kelly's Koffee Shop, the first in the Cedar Bay Cozy Mystery Series), for becoming a dog that I can finally trust when she's quiet! Believe me, that took a little time. Thanks, Kelly!

Amazing Ebooks & Paperbacks for FREE

Go to www.dianneharman.com/freepaperback.html and get your FREE copies of Dianne's books and Dianne's favorite recipes immediately by signing up for her newsletter.

Once you've signed up for her newsletter you're eligible to win autographed paperbacks. One lucky winner is picked every week. Hurry before the offer ends.

PROLOGUE

The High Desert Country Music Festival is held in the Spring of every year at the White Stallion Ranch outside of Palm Springs, California. The event is hard to describe. It's a lot easier to experience it. Reminiscent of the 1969 Woodstock Festival, the youth of today come in large numbers, some with flowers in their hair and stars in their eyes, some looking for romance, some looking for a meaningful experience, and others simply wanting to be part of the action, whatever it might be. The preferred dress for men is jeans and a bare chest, while Daisy Mae shorts and a tank top is the standard dress for women. Many of the festival attendees wear cowboy boots, belts with big silver buckles, and cowboy hats. While the Palm Springs area is not considered "country," the wannabes all play the part for the weekend.

Like anything else, there's a flip side, a dark side if you will, to the festival. Drugs are rampant, and the festival food and drinks don't come cheap. Beer and Fireball whiskey are the drinks of choice while molly capsules are the drug of choice. Who knew the dark side would include the murder of a once famous television chef making a comeback after spending several years in seclusion?

CHAPTER ONE

Darkness had settled over the high desert area located not far from Palm Springs, California. In a small residential compound owned by Laura James, a modern day psychic who worked for an insurance company, six friends were enjoying dinner in the courtyard under a large spreading tree strung with twinkling lights that made the setting almost magical. John Anderson, the portly affable owner of The Red Pony food truck, regularly prepared dinners and tried out some of his new recipes on the people who lived in the four houses that formed the compound. Included in the group that evening was a soon-to-be permanent addition to the group, Detective Jeff Combs of the Palm Springs Police Department. He and Laura's sister, Marty Morgan, had recently announced their plans to get married in a few months.

Marty had accepted Laura's invitation to move to California from her long-time home in the Midwest and take up residence in the compound after her husband, Scott Morgan, had asked for a divorce so he could marry his long-time secretary. Marty was an art and antique appraiser, and through Laura's insurance connections she'd started an appraisal practice in the desert. Over the last year she'd developed a very good reputation and had become highly sought-after as an appraiser of personal property. Laura's long-time boyfriend, Les Anderson, a well-known artist, and John's assistant at The Red Pony, Max Samuels, rounded out the group that had gathered in the courtyard that evening.

As usual, they shared a glass of wine and discussed the events of the day, while John and Max brought out the food for the evening's dinner. Max worked for John and helped him prep the food truck for the following day. He was pretty much a regular dinner guest at the compound.

"Max and I've been so busy today getting the food ready for the High Desert Country Music Festival, and at the same time setting up The Red Pony for lunch, that I didn't have time to fix a special dinner tonight," John said. "These are some of the things I'll be serving at the festival. Since it's a country western festival, I'm serving food I think will fit in well with the theme. I really appreciate it that all of you have volunteered to help me out during the festival. I'm kind of nervous about it, since I've never done an event that large. I just hope I have enough food and that people like what's on the menu."

"John, where is the Pony physically going to be set up at the festival?" Les asked.

"Fortunately, I've got what I think is an excellent spot. I'm the first food truck on the left when people enter the food truck court. Even if they don't buy anything, I'll be the first truck they see when they come in and the last one they see when they leave. If nothing else, it's got to be good advertising for The Red Pony."

He stopped talking and answered his ringing phone which was playing the song, Country Roads. "John Anderson, here." He stood up from the picnic table where the group was seated and walked away from it, as he listened to the voice on the other end. He waved his hand indicating that the others should start eating without him. A few moments later he returned, his face twisted and red with anger.

"I don't believe this. I've been telling you about this guy named Jacques Ruchon who got kicked off that food television show a few years ago," he said, sitting back down at the table. "He went into seclusion, as he calls it, for a couple of years, although others have insinuated he went into rehab to deal with his drug habit. Recently he started a food truck business called French Food Obsession. His truck always seems to be near mine at lunchtime. It's like he's trying to horn in on The Red Pony's business. Now I find out that Rocco, the owner of the Italian Stallion food truck, and the person who was going to be parked next to me at the festival, is sick and won't be bringing his truck to the festival.

"The person in charge of the food trucks put Jacques' truck next to mine," he fumed. "For three days I'm going to more or less have to share space with him, and I hate the guy. I've always suspected he isn't really French. I spent a little time in Paris attending a cooking school, and his accent sure doesn't sound like what I heard when I was there. I bet he paid off the festival promoter so he could park next to The Red Pony, because he wants to steal my clientele."

"I can't believe he'd be a threat to your business," Laura said. "You've developed a cult following of foodies in the area. He shouldn't be a problem. Remember, most of the people who will be there are young, and your food is going to appeal to them a lot more than French food, plus, all of the employees at the insurance company where I work swear by your food. They love it."

"Thanks for trying to make me feel better," John said. "I wish I could believe you, but I'd bet my last dollar that he has some sneaky reason for wanting to park his truck next to mine. He's one of the few people I know that if something bad happened to him, I wouldn't feel the least bit sorry. I'd like him to just go away and get out of my life. In fact, I'd probably celebrate if something bad actually did happen to him."

"I'm right there with you, Boss," Max said, "but right now we got other things to worry about. Forget Jacques. He ain't worth your time. We need to get all the supplies up to that building the owner of the ranch is letting us use. I'm glad it's got a walk-in refrigerator. We're gonna need it."

"I'm planning on doing that after dinner, so we can use tomorrow morning for last minute packing and getting the motor homes loaded."

"John, what do you want us to do tomorrow?" Jeff asked.

"We need to get out to the festival grounds about 9:00 in the morning, so I can be ready when the festival opens at noon. Marty, I'd appreciate it if you would drive Jeff and Max to the motor home rental place about 7:30. I've reserved two motor homes. There's one for the four of you and one for Max and me. Jeff and Max can drive the motor homes to the compound, and we'll load them up with the food I'll be needing.

"I'd like to convoy to the festival. We'll get there early, and the event planner guaranteed me two parking spots for the motor homes right behind where The Red Pony will be located in the food court. I'll drive the Pony in, and Max and Jeff can park the motor homes in our assigned spots. Even though we have assigned spots, I don't want any last minute glitches, and that's why I'd like us to drive out to the festival in a convoy. At least we'll be together if there's a problem. I just hope they haven't assigned the spots next to our motor homes to Jacques and his group."

"I'm excited," Marty said. "This is a first for me. I've never been to a music festival before. I'm sure I speak for all of us, John, when I say just let us know what you want us to do, and we'll see that it gets done. Now if you'll excuse me, I need to pack and make sure I have everything ready to go. I'm taking Duke to Lucy's home early tomorrow morning. You all know her. She's the one who works at the Hi-Lo Drug Store. Jeff, if you're ready to leave, I'll walk you out to your car."

"Yes, I need to go home and pack," the large middle-aged detective said. Even though Marty's fiancé was greying at the temples, he was still a very handsome man. From the looks he received when they were out together, she knew she wasn't the only woman who felt that he was quite attractive. The thing that had originally attracted her to Jeff was his smile. Her love of it hadn't diminished with time. It lit up his whole face and never failed to make her smile in return.

As was his custom when he didn't have his pink booties on, Duke,

Marty's loveable but sometimes neurotic black Labrador dog, stopped at the gate while Jeff and Marty walked over to his car, arms around one another as they shared a goodnight kiss. "See you in the morning, handsome," she said.

CHAPTER TWO

The next morning John stopped The Red Pony at the entrance gate leading to the festival parking lot and showed his vehicle pass to the attendant. She looked at it and the two motor homes that were following him and waved them through. In the distance they saw a big sign that said "Food Truck Court." John stopped his truck, jumped out of the cab, and walked back to the two motor homes.

"We've got the original spaces they gave me. I'm going through the gate that leads to the food court with the Pony, and I'll park it on the left side. You can both park your motor homes on the other side of the fence behind the Pony. That'll make it real easy for me to get some of those dry food items and the extra things I packed in the refrigerators and storage areas in your motor homes. When you get parked, come on in. Since the food court isn't open to the public until noon, tell the attendant at the gate that you're with The Red Pony. Shouldn't be a problem. See you in a few minutes."

Laura, Les, Marty, Jeff, and Max told the attendant they were with The Red Pony and walked over to it. The space reserved for the French Food Obsession was empty. They helped John set up the awning which he hoped would provide enough shade to keep the area near The Red Pony bearable in the spring desert heat.

A few minutes later a handsome dark-haired man maneuvered a food truck bearing the name "French Food Obsession" into the empty space next to John's truck. When John realized Jacques had arrived, he visibly tensed up, but then he resumed getting ready for the crowd that would soon be descending on the food trucks once the festival gates opened. A few moments later there was a knock on the bottom half of the Pony's dutch door.

"Bon jour, John, I see that we are to be neighbors, oui?" Jacques asked.

John walked over to the door and answered coldly, "Yeah, it looks like it."

"Well, it's probably time for you to see how a real chef cooks. Maybe that's why we were parked next to each other, so you could learn from a master. Good luck. I have to go back to the Obsession and prepare for the crowds that I'm sure are going to love my food," he said as he walked back to his truck.

John turned and faced his friends who were clearly shocked by what Jacques had just said. "See why I'd like to see the guy planted in the ground? Now you understand what I have to go through each time I see him," John said. He was so angry he was visibly shaking.

"Getting angry isn't going to do you one bit of good, John," Marty said. "You've got a lot more important things to do right now than worrying about that jerk, and by the way, I happen to agree with your assessment of his French heritage. I think he's about as French as I am. When I was in college I spent a semester in Paris studying antiques and art. There is definitely something off about his accent, but none of that really matters now. What's important is that you're all set up and ready to go when the swarms of hungry people come through the gate. Let's forget about him and get started."

It was apparent to all of them that John was having a very hard time turning his attention back to the business at hand in the Pony, but within a few minutes he'd given each of them a "to-do" list, and they spent the rest of the morning getting ready for the crowds that were expected to descend on the food truck when the gate opened at noon.

Jeff and Marty had been given the task of getting the sit-down eating area ready next to the truck. The festival promoter had provided plastic tables and chairs which they set up under the awning. Laura had purchased several bunches of flowers and they made floral arrangements for each of the tables by first putting rocks and water in large plastic cups and then placing some brightly colored red flowers in each of the cups. The red and white motif played perfectly off of the fire engine red color of The Red Pony. They placed napkin dispensers and salt and pepper shakers on the tables, finishing up a few minutes before the first of the festival attendees would be entering the food court area.

John walked out of the truck with some chalk and a menu list written on a piece of paper. "Jeff would you write the menu on the chalkboard next to the window? Here's what we'll be serving," he said as he handed the list of Jeff. "I want the people to start thinking about the food they can order. Thanks," he said as he hurried back into the Pony.

Jeff looked at the list and said, "Don't know about the customers, but my mouth is watering just looking at this menu." The food John was serving at The Red Pony was comfort food with a country flavor, sure to appeal to the large crowd which had lined up at the gate, wanting to be the first to sample the foods from the different trucks.

Marty nodded her approval as Jeff began to list the items being served: brisket of beef sandwich, pork ribs, ham steak with red eye gravy, coleslaw, barbecue beans, chicken fried steak with cornmeal hush puppies and gravy, ranch style eggs on a bacon waffle, watermelon, and oatmeal cookies. Marty thought the cold long neck beer bottles that the festival attendees could buy at the nearby beer stands along with John's food was bound to meet with the approval of the young festival attendees.

She looked over at the French Food Obsession truck which was painted in a soft green color with accents of pale watery blues and milky whites reminiscent of the colors used in a French country kitchen. The inside of the truck was painted white and the window where orders were placed and served had a charming green and white striped awning over it. Gleaming copper pans hanging on pegs inside the truck could be seen through the window.

Next to the window was a menu written in green chalk on a white chalkboard. Just as John had chosen to do, Jacques had limited his selection to ten items, and he had carefully translated them into English, since all of them were classic French dishes.

"I don't want to be disloyal to John," Marty said, "but that menu really looks good to me, however, from the age of the people I see standing outside the gate, I can't believe many of them are going to be interested in Jacques' food. Seems more like the type of food people our age would eat. I can't help but think John's truck is going to do a much better business with his western style food."

"I agree. It's close to opening time, so we better see what else John wants us to do."

CHAPTER THREE

When Marty and Jeff walked into the Red Pony to find out what else John needed them to do, they heard Max say, "Boss, let it go. I'd like to see the guy six feet under, too, but the fact is the jerk is gonna be next to us for the entire weekend, and we gotta concentrate on those people outside the gate who are gonna want some good western food in a few minutes. Let's give the people what they want. Come on, John, don't let this guy get to you. He ain't worth it."

"If his truck does better than mine I'll personally walk next door and bury my best chopping knife in the middle of his forehead."

"John, I heard that," Jeff said. "If you keep talking like that and anything happens to Jacques, you might find yourself in trouble. You don't want anyone to overhear you saying things like that. We're all set up outside. What else do you want us to do?"

John looked around and said, "I think I'd like you both to keep the outside eating area picked up. There's nothing worse than a lot of trash on the ground next to a food truck. There's some big trash bins behind the beer bar in the center of the food truck court, plus I brought a couple of extra ones and put them behind the Pony. Max and I will be using those, so if you could dump them from time to time that would be a big help.

"Les, Laura, I'd like you to do whatever Max and I might ask you to do. Could be anything from getting more bread out of one of the motor homes to helping us serve at the window. Just stand by and be ready for whatever comes up. Okay, guys," he said, looking at his watch. "It's show time! The gates just opened, and The Red Pony is officially open for business."

The afternoon and night went by in a blur for Marty. She couldn't believe how much trash people threw on the ground. Her back was beginning to talk to her from bending over. It seemed like wherever she looked she saw people drinking from flasks and appearing happier than she thought the music would have made them. The line at The Red Pony was steady from the moment they opened, but what surprised her was the number of people standing in line at the French Food Obsession truck. Several times she noticed a stunning young blond woman standing in line and thought she must be getting food for people and taking it to them. There was no way she could eat that much food by herself.

Marty was cleaning off a couple of the tables outside The Red Pony when she saw John gesturing to her, indicating he wanted her to come into the Pony and talk to him. She walked in and said, "Looks like it's going great. Think you brought enough food?"

"Yeah, we're doing fine, but I'd like to know what Jacques is serving. Do me a favor and copy his menu down for me, would you? I'm curious about what he's serving."

Marty left the truck and waved to Jeff who was pulling an overflowing trash barrel towards the large bins in the center of the food truck court. "Back in a minute."

"Where are you off to?" Jeff asked.

"John wants me to go next door to the French Food Obsession and see what Jacques is serving."

"Well, whatever it is, they're definitely buying. In fact, I've noticed a couple of them have been there more than once, like that drop-dead gorgeous young blond woman," he said as he nodded towards the long line in front of the French Food Obsession.

"Jeff, are you focusing on beautiful young women instead of doing what John's asked you to do?" Marty asked, with a twinkle in her eye.

"Nope. I'm doing everything he's asked, but when you see the same spectacular looking woman go to a food truck for the third time, you have to wonder if she has a thing for Jacques or what. Look over there. She's the fourth one from the front of the line. You can't miss her."

Marty looked over at the line in front of the French Food Obsession and saw one of the most beautiful young women she'd ever seen. She was talking animatedly to the person standing behind her. Her long blond hair set off a perfectly tanned body that indicated it had spent a lot of time with a personal trainer. Jade colored green eyes were enhanced by her tan. She wore short cut-off jeans which accentuated her long legs. A sleeveless cropped white tank top showed off her tan midriff and pierced belly button. Gold hoop earrings and a gold necklace completed the modern day Daisy Mae look.

"Detective, hate to say this, but you're old enough to be her father. Guess she just likes French food."

"You're probably right, but the whole thing strikes me as a bit odd, but then again, I've never been to one of these music festivals before."

Marty walked next door to where the French Food Obsession truck was parked and stood off to the side of the line. She wrote down what Jacques had written on the chalk board and looked at it again to make sure she'd gotten it right.

This is bizarre. This food might appeal to people of my age who are dining in an expensive fancy French restaurant but here at the festival? I can't believe all these young people are standing in line for food like this. It makes absolutely no sense to me.

She walked back to the Pony and stepped inside. John was busy cooking and said, "Tell me what's on the list. I can't take time to read it."

"Okay, here goes. I wrote it down exactly like it is on his menu. I think I can pronounce everything, but cut me a little slack if I make a mistake." Marty looked at her list and said, "croissant jambon sandwich (ham), quiche Lorraine, baked Camembert, hachis Parmentier (French version of shepherd's pie), steak tartare (a French delicacy), cassoulet (French casserole with beans and chicken), pissaladiere (French pizza), aligot (mashed potatoes with melted cheese and garlic), gougeres (cream puffs), and crème brulee (French custard). He's put explanations for most of the dishes in parentheses next to the name of the dish."

"You've got to be kidding me," John exclaimed. "The only thing I can see any of these young people being remotely interested in would be the French pizza. What's going on? I really can't figure it out. I'm doing almost all of the cooking, so I can't see much of what's happening over there. Is anybody buying his food?"

"Yes. The line in front of his truck is quite long." She didn't want to tell him it was much longer than the one at The Red Pony.

"Marty, do you think he knows you're helping me?" John asked.

"I have no idea. Why?"

"I'd like you to stand in line over there and order something. See if you overhear anything that might indicate why so many people are standing in a long line to buy his food. Can you do that?"

"I can try. I'll be back in a few minutes. If Jeff wonders where I am, tell him what I'm doing."

"Thanks. By the way, don't eat whatever you get. I want to see what it looks and tastes like."

CHAPTER FOUR

When Marty went next door to the French Food Obsession she had to stand in line for nearly thirty minutes. By now it was eight at night, and she was exhausted. The sun had set, and the festival was ablaze with lights. Most of the food trucks had been strung with twinkling lights all around them as well as lights on their canopies. She heard various kinds of music floating through the air. As she looked around, she felt like she was in a contrived fairyland, something quite surreal.

When she was getting close to the front of the line she heard angry voices coming from behind the French Food Obsession. "Give me what you've got. You know how much you owe me," a woman's voice said in an angry tone.

A man answered in a thick French accent, "Get out of here. I don't have time for this now. When this weekend is over, we'll talk."

"No, that's what you always say, and it never happens. You're so far behind on the child support you owe me, I should probably go to the district attorney and have you arrested, and you'd never cook again. What are you going to spend your money on? Same thing you always do?"

"If you don't leave now, I'll call the police and have you arrested for disturbing the peace. Every minute I'm not cooking costs us both. Come back tonight after midnight, and I'll pay you what I can. This is not the time nor the place for this conversation."

"All right, but this time you better keep your promise, or you'll regret it for the rest of your life, which may very well wind up being a lot shorter than you thought it was going to be."

"Jennifer, are you threatening me?" the man Marty assumed was Jacques Ruchon asked.

"Call it whatever you like. I'll see you later."

A moment later a woman walked out from behind the truck, clearly agitated. Her face was red, and her eyes were flashing. She cut in front of Marty as she walked towards the central part of the food truck court. Marty looked around, but no one seemed at all interested in the woman. It was as if Marty was the only one who'd heard the angry exchange of words. The young man in front of her ordered the quiche Lorraine special. When she got to the front of the line, a smiling Jacques asked her what she would like. She ordered the hachis Parmentier. As she was walking away, she heard the person behind her order the cassoulet special.

That's weird. I wrote down all the items on the menu for John, and I don't recall seeing the word special on anything. I must have missed it, or maybe the people who have been to his food truck before get something a little different when they say the word "special." It's probably like when I go to my favorite hamburger place and order my burger "animal style." It's kind of an inside thing, and I love the grilled onions which is what animal style means.

She carried her plate with the hachis Parmentier in a tin foil type soup bowl into John's truck. He looked at it and grimaced. He took a bite and said, "That fake French jerk has his nerve. That's plain old shepherd's pie, and it has very little meat in it. What did he charge you for that drek?"

"I paid $7.95 for it."

"You're kidding me! That's highway robbery! It's just a few

vegetables and a couple of pieces of meat in a gravy covered with mashed potatoes. It couldn't cost him more than fifty cents, if that, to make. That's one heck of a markup."

"I wouldn't know about that. However, while I was standing in line I heard an argument between a woman and a man, who I'm pretty sure was Jacques, arguing about some back child support he owed her. Do you know anything about that?"

John took a long drink from the water bottle that was next to him. He wiped the back of his hand across his forehead, clearly tired. "Sorry, Marty, but I'm whipped. I can't wait until it's time to close the Pony, and I can get some much-needed sleep. The last few days have been exhausting for me. Anyway, let me answer your question. I've heard rumors that he owes his ex-wife a lot of money, but I don't know that for sure. I would imagine it's probably true. Rumor also has it that the reason he never could pay her what he owed her, was because he spent all his money on drugs, but I can't say that for certain either. The restaurant business is a hotbed of rumors, most of which aren't true. That may be one of them. Since I'm not at all close to the guy, nor do I want to be, I don't know anything about his ex-wife. I do know he's divorced, and he's the father of a fourteen-year-old boy. That's about the sum total of what I know of his personal life, which really isn't that much."

"After I heard the two of them arguing, I was curious what you might know about him. Evidently she's coming back to meet him after the festival closes tonight to discuss it further. Oh, one other question. I never saw the word 'special' on Jacques' menu, but the young man in front of me ordered a special and the young woman behind me did too. Is that some kind of an inside thing?" Marty asked.

"Could be. I don't know anything about it."

"Let me turn to another subject. I understand the owner of the White Stallion Ranch where this festival is being held is Jeb Rhodes. I also read that he loves country music, and that's one of the reasons he started holding the festival on his property, not too far from his ranch house. There's a big house up on that knoll you can see from here, and I'll bet that's his ranch house. The reason I'm bringing it up is because I got a call from a Jeb Rhodes a few days ago asking me to give him a call. Evidently he has an extensive collection of California Impressionist paintings he'd like me to appraise. I was so busy finishing up an appraisal I was working on and getting ready for the festival, that I never had a chance to return his call. I thought I'd take a break and walk over to the ranch house. Maybe he's there, and we can talk about his collection. Would that be okay with you?"

"Absolutely. As hard as you've been working you definitely deserve a break. See you in a little while."

"I don't see Jeff. Would you tell him where I've gone?"

"Of course. Good luck with getting the appraisal," John said as he turned back to the griddle and looked at the orders Laura had placed next to where he and Max were cooking. He quickly directed his attention to preparing the orders, as Marty stepped out of the food truck.

CHAPTER FIVE

Marty walked out of the food truck court and into the main area of the festival where several large sound stages had been set up. There were several large tents, and the music coming from all of them blended into the central area. She looked around wide-eyed at the mass of young people milling around in the open area outside the tents, some clearly showing the effects of substances that were supposed to be banned from the festival. The crowd was a moving swaying mass of humanity.

She walked to the far side of the main area and showed her pass to the guard at the gate. "I have business with Jeb Rhodes at his ranch house. I'll be back in a little while." She walked up the tree-lined driveway to where the large rambling one-story ranch house was located. As she approached it, she heard a loud angry voice coming from the porch, so she stepped behind a tree, not wanting to draw attention to herself.

"Brianna, you're buzzed," a man's voice said. "Get in the house. I can tell you're on something. Where did you find it? Is someone selling stuff at the festival? I know other festivals have had problems in the past, but I hired extra guards, so there wouldn't be a drug problem at my festival. Obviously they're not doing their job if my own daughter can get them. Where did you get them?"

As she peered around the tree, Marty saw an older man grab the young woman's arm and pull her through the front door. Marty gasped as she realized it was the beautiful young woman Jeff had pointed out earlier in the day. She could clearly see the young woman because of the light shining through the doorway. Marty heard the man continue to talk loudly to the young woman. "You tell me now where you got the drugs, or you won't leave this house again for a month. Hear me, Brianna? I've had enough of this."

The man was quiet for a moment and Marty assumed the girl he called Brianna was talking. After a few minutes, she heard him say, "You promised me you'd never take a molly again, and now you're saying you got them from someone who's working at the festival. Tell me who, and I'll make sure that he never sells another one as long as he's alive. In fact, I might just be inclined to kill the scumbag who has the nerve to sell drugs at my festival which has been widely promoted as being a drug free event.

'I never thought I'd say that I'm glad your mother isn't here to see what you've become, but right now I am. It would break her heart to see her daughter in your condition. If you expect to get any type of an inheritance from me, this better never happen again. I'm tempted to put you into a drug rehab facility. Maybe that would keep you off of drugs."

The man who Marty assumed was Jeb Rhodes became quiet, and she could hear a soft voice talking, but couldn't make out the words. She waited for what seemed an eternity and then the front door opened wider and the older man came out on the porch, a cell phone in his hand. "Sid, I've got a little job for you to do tonight. I found out that one of the people who's working here at the festival is selling a drug called molly to people, but I don't know exactly who it is. I can't have that. If word gets out they're available, and combined with the heat and the music, if they take that drug we could have people dying like they did at that electronic music festival in New York a few years ago. Not on my watch. I'll do whatever it takes to make sure that doesn't happen. Here's what I want you to do," he said as his voice trailed off when he closed the door and walked back inside the house.

Well, this probably isn't the right time to knock on the door and talk to him about his California Impressionist painting collection. Think that will have to wait until the festival is over. I'll give him a call next week.

Marty turned, walked back down the driveway, and re-entered the festival, wondering if the young people she had noticed earlier who looked like they were under the influence of something had been sold mollies as well.

Jeff is extremely opposed to drugs and with his background in law enforcement, I wonder if he's noticed anything. Surely he's aware that some of these kids are showing the effects of substance abuse. I wonder what he'd make of the conversation I just overheard between Brianna and her father. I'll tell him after we finish up tonight. Right now I probably better get back and see what I can do to help John. Bet Laura's whipped by now. Taking orders for that long has got to be exhausting. I'll offer to do it tomorrow.

I've never felt particularly old before, but I must be getting that way, because I don't understand how these young people can listen to this music all day in this heat. All I want right now is some peace and quiet.

CHAPTER SIX

"Okay, guys, they just closed the gates," John said as he turned off the stove top burners and the oven. "It's been an incredibly long day. I can't thank you enough for all your help. Give Max and me a few minutes to clean up this mess in the kitchen, and then let's all meet at my motor home for a glass of wine before we crash for the night."

"Sounds good to me," Laura said. "I was getting to the point if I had to look at one more barbecued beef sandwich I was afraid I'd throw up and figured that wouldn't be very good for business."

"Laura, I've already decided I'll take the counter tomorrow. You can help Jeff with the outside stuff," Marty said.

"Don't need to ask me twice. I gratefully accept," she said as she untied her apron that was smeared with bits of the food she'd served all day.

"Give your apron to me, Laura," John said. "I'll put it in my motor home. I have fresh ones for tomorrow. See you guys in about fifteen minutes. Come on Max, let's get this over with."

Laura, Les, Marty, and Jeff walked out of the food truck court into the parking lot and over to where their motor home was parked. The back door of The Red Pony was open, and they could see Max and John finishing up the last of the dirty pots and pans.

"How about if I pour everyone a glass of wine, and we can take it with us over to John's when he gets there? I could use one now," Les said.

The other three nodded their heads in agreement. A few minutes later, wine glass in hand, Marty said, "I knew this was going to be an adventure, but it's turning out to be a lot of things I wasn't expecting. I'd heard that security is very strict about drugs not being allowed at the festival, but from what I've seen today, it looks like someone didn't get the message. Jeff, what's your professional law enforcement take on it? Then I want to tell you about an experience I had a little while ago."

"Law enforcement has known about the problem of drugs at these musical festivals for years," Jeff said. "Every law enforcement person is well aware of the deadly combination of drugs and heat, often with alcohol added to the mix. In fact, a lot of Palm Springs police officers are working here undercover on their days off from the department. I've recognized several today, and yes, from what I've observed, the young people in attendance are definitely getting drugs from somewhere."

"Before I tell you about a conversation I overheard, are you familiar with something called a molly?" Marty asked him.

"Yeah, it's pretty much the drug of choice at today's music festivals. Actually the drug has been around for a long time, but twenty or thirty years ago it was called ecstasy. The term 'molly' is just the street name for the drug being sold today. It's very appealing to people at this type of a venue because they feel euphoric and a sense of closeness to all the people around them."

"It's hard to think of a dangerous drug being called molly," Les said.

"Which is exactly why people started calling it that. Talk on the street is that it's purer than other drugs, not contaminated so to speak, but that's not true. You really don't know what you're getting. The government has classified it as a Schedule One drug which means it has no accepted medical use and a high probability of misuse. It's on the same plane as heroin. My guess is we might see some problems tomorrow if this heat keeps up. The combination of excessive heat and the drug can literally be deadly." Jeff turned to Marty and said, "Where did you ever hear the term molly?"

"About eight tonight I walked up to the ranch house on the knoll. John may have told you that the owner of the ranch, Jeb Rhodes, left a telephone message for me a few days ago about possibly hiring me to appraise his California Impressionist art collection. When I got there here's what happened." She told them about what she had heard Jeb Rhodes saying and later about his telephone call to someone named Sid. "Jeff, that beautiful blond you pointed out to me earlier today is his daughter, Brianna. I was able to get a very good look at her. From everything her father said and what she evidently told him, looks like the drug molly is being sold here at the festival."

"I wouldn't be the least bit surprised," Jeff said. "The problem is figuring out who's selling it. It could be anyone at the festival, band members, vendors, attendees, guards, anyone. It's really like trying to find a needle in a haystack. The question is, where do you start?"

"Quiet, everybody. I'm hearing loud voices. I know it's still hotter than blazes, but I'm sure I hear something. I'm going to open the door a bit," Laura said.

CHAPTER SEVEN

Laura stood up and walked over to the door. When she opened it the four of them heard loud music coming from The Red Pony. Along with the music, men's raised voices could be heard.

"Shhh," Laura said. "I want to see if I can make out what's being said." They listened for several minutes, and then the voices became quieter. She looked at the other three and said, "I don't feel good about this. I sense something is wrong. Could you make out anything?"

"Maybe," Marty said, "but I don't think the voices were coming from The Red Pony. I think they were coming from the French Food Obsession truck or just behind it. I could be wrong, but it sounded like someone said, "You owe me more than this. I brought you the stuff. I can't wait any longer for the money."

"Did you hear what the other voice said?" Jeff asked."

"No, and I'm not sure if I was imagining it, but I'd almost swear the voice had a French accent, like Jacques'."

"Maybe it was him. Could you make anything else out?" Les asked.

"It sounded like the person said, 'I promised you I'd pay, and I will. Give me a few more hours. Now let me have that bag.' Then I thought I heard someone running. Of course it all could have been my imagination."

Laura closed the motor home door, and they were quiet for a few moments, trying to absorb and understand what had just happened. The music that had been playing at The Red Pony had been turned off. They became aware of French music coming from the French Food Obsession truck.

Jeff turned to Laura and said, "Laura, you're the resident psychic here. Are you picking up on anything?"

To a bystander, the words directed to the attractive middle-aged woman would have seemed ridiculous. No crystal balls, flowing skirts, or mumbo jumbo were evident. Laura wore jeans and a sleeveless white shirt. Her dark hair was pulled back and held in place by a large silver barrette. She looked far more like the mother of one of the festival attendees than a psychic, but that's what she was. When she had been a student at UCLA she'd taken part in an experimental study to determine if certain people had psychic abilities. No one could explain it, but Laura was found by the professors conducting the experiment at the university to have extremely high levels of intuitiveness and extra sensory perception.

She had used her powers to help Marty and Jeff solve murder cases in the past, and while Marty had been aware of Laura's gift from the time she was a little girl, Jeff had only recently become a firm believer in her abilities. Laura took a deep breath and began to speak. "Jeff, I don't think I've ever said this before, but I'm getting a definite sense that a murder is going to take place in the very near future. None of us will be the victim, but we will be involved, and that includes John and Max. I'm sorry, I wish I could be more specific, but that's all I'm getting."

"Laura, you know I trust your intuition, and what you're saying really makes me nervous. Is there anything we can do to prevent it? Is there anything else you can tell us?" Jeff asked.

"I don't know if it's because we heard the music coming from the French Food Obsession truck, but I feel it has something to do with that truck. Oh, here come John and Max. Let's not say anything to them. They have enough on their minds without getting bogged down in something like this."

Les walked over to the door and answered the knock. "John, we'll come over to your motor home in just a minute. Afraid we started without you and Max. Hope you don't mind."

"No problem. I would have too." John said as he and Max walked to their motor home and started the air conditioner. The four others followed.

"Well, what do you think of the festival so far?" John asked as he poured them each a glass of wine.

"We were just talking about it. Looks to us like there might be some illegal substances being consumed," Les said.

"From what I know of music festivals, and although I've never worked one, I've been to a couple, and that's pretty much the usual case. Even though people's backpacks and purses are searched by security, it's easy to bring the stuff in. I could have brought in enough drugs in the food truck and the motor home to insure I'd never have to work another day in my life if I sold them all. This is kind of the way it is at these types of festivals. Don't forget, with the price of the tickets, beer, and food, everyone who comes here has to have a little money. It's not a far stretch of the imagination to figure they're spending a little more of it on recreational drugs. They come for the total experience, not to just see one band."

"I'm sure you're right," Laura said. "To change the subject, how did you do today? Was it profitable for you?"

"Very, and I wasn't even price-gouging like Jacques was. I still can't figure out why the line for his food was so long. Marty bought the hachis Parmentier for me, and it was actually one of the worst renditions of shepherd's pie I've ever had. Marty said a lot of people

27

were ordering it. I can't figure it out."

"At $7.95, I can't either," Marty said as she stood up. "If you all want to stay and party, feel free to. I'm whipped, and I need to get some sleep, or I won't be any help to anyone tomorrow."

"Think I can speak for all of us," Laura said. "We'll join you."

"John, I understand that the festival doesn't open until noon tomorrow. Why don't I fix breakfast for all of us around ten?" Marty said.

"That would be much appreciated," John said. "I love to cook but with these crowds and in this heat, if I had to do breakfast as well, think it would be a total burn-out for me. See you at ten."

Jeff, Marty, Les, and Laura walked next door to their motor home unaware of what was taking place in Jacques' motor home located just a few feet away and how it would affect each of them.

CHAPTER EIGHT

At nine on Saturday morning Marty woke up and heard a lot of commotion coming from Jacques' motor home which was behind the French Food Obsession truck. She looked out the window and screamed, "Oh no, the paramedics are taking a body out of Jacques' motor home, and it's covered with a sheet." By the time she'd finished speaking, Jeff had pulled on his jeans and a t-shirt and was hurrying out the door. The three remaining occupants of the motor home saw him talking to the paramedics while several men in sheriff's uniforms arrived. People were gathering around the motor home, and the already crowded parking lot was becoming even more crowded as people streamed in to see what had happened.

Marty, Laura, and Les watched the scene that was taking place in front of them with a sense of disbelief. Marty recognized Ned Billings, who was the sous chef at the French Food Obsession. He was talking to the sheriff's deputies and gesturing and pointing at the motor home occupied by John and Max. Neither one of them could be seen as they apparently were still sleeping, unaware of the drama that was playing out in the parking lot. Jeff stood off to one side, taking it all in. When Ned stopped talking, they saw Jeff walk up to the man in a sheriff's uniform who appeared to be in charge and show the man his identification. They spoke for a few minutes and then Jeff walked back to their motor home and stepped inside.

"What's going on?" Marty asked.

"Looks like Jacques was murdered sometime last night. Since the murder happened in his motor home the sheriff's deputies have yellow taped it as a crime scene, but they told Jacques' assistant, guess his name is Ned Billings, that he could open the French Food Obsession for business today, but here's the bad thing. Ned accused John and Max of murdering his boss. He said it was pretty common knowledge John hated Jacques because John felt he was some kind of threatening competition."

"No," Laura said. "That's not true. Neither John nor Max did it. I know that. You all know about my psychic ability, and I know that neither one of them murdered Jacques."

"I believe you, but I'm not sure the sheriff will. This is county land and the sheriff has jurisdiction over the case. He's on his way here right now. His deputy wants to take statements from all of us, since our motor home is next to Jacques'."

"John and Max need to be told. I'll go over there now," Laura said. "Better they hear it from me than from the sheriff."

"I'm going with you. I want to tell them not to say anything that could in any way be incriminating," Jeff said.

"This is ridiculous," Marty said. "We were with John and Max last night."

"Technically, you're right, sweetheart, but the sheriff's response might very well be that we don't know what they did after we left their motor home."

"This is plain wrong. There must be some other reason why Jacques was murdered. Remember, there was that argument with his ex-wife and also the incident I saw up at the ranch house."

"Marty," Jeff said. "Let me give you some advice. I think you'd be far better off not to point your finger at anyone. When you give them your statement you can say you heard nothing coming from the motor home, and that's the truth."

"Well, what about the raised voices we heard last night coming from behind the French Food Obsession truck? Maybe whoever Jacques was talking to is the one who killed him."

"Trust me, Marty. At this point don't say anything," Jeff said in a cautionary tone of voice. "Let's see what happens in the next couple of hours. Come on Laura, we really need to go over to John and Max's motor home and tell them what happened."

After Jeff and Laura left, Marty looked out the window of their motor home and said, "Look, Les, that's Jeb Rhodes, the owner of the White Stallion Ranch. He must have been notified. Love to know what he's saying to the deputies."

"We'll probably find out real soon. Looks like Jeff left John's and is listening to them. Now he's talking to the deputy. Uh-oh, Jeff is walking over here, and a deputy's with him. We better get dressed."

Jeff opened the door and without going inside said in a loud voice, "Deputy Ormsby is with me. He wants to take our statements. Open the door when you're dressed. I'm going to stay outside with him."

A few minutes later Marty opened the door and said, "We're dressed, Deputy, please come in."

"I won't take up much of your time, ma'am, but I'd like you to tell me if you heard or saw anything strange going on at Mr. Ruchon's motor home last night." Over the deputy's shoulder, Les and Marty could see Jeff almost imperceptibly shaking his head, indicating they were to say nothing.

They told the deputy they had a glass of wine at John's motor home and then returned to their motor home and were asleep within minutes.

"That's the same thing Detective Combs said." He turned to Jeff, "I assume if I talk to the fourth person," he looked at his notes and resumed speaking, "Laura James, she'll corroborate what you've told me."

"I'm sure she will, because that's what happened."

"Okay, thanks for your statements. I'll get one from her later. I need to go next door and get statements from the two men who worked at The Red Pony."

"Deputy Ormsby, I think Laura's next door with John and Max, so you can get her statement when you talk to the two of them. Do you see any reason why The Red Pony can't open for business today?" Marty asked.

"Not unless one of those men tells me he killed Mr. Ruchon and hid the murder weapon in The Red Pony," he said laughing. "Again, thanks for your time."

"Deputy, I'll go over there with you. Might make it a little easier for them," Jeff said.

The deputy looked at him shrewdly. "If you weren't a law enforcement person, it would almost seem to me like you want to be there to make sure they don't say anything incriminating to me."

"Not at all," Jeff said smoothly. "These are my friends, and they're under enough stress just trying to cook for all the festival guests. I thought my being there with you would make it a little less stressful for them."

Jeff turned back to Les and Marty. "Marty, why don't you come over in a couple of minutes and get the key to The Red Pony. I think you need to open it up, and then you and Laura probably need to get started on the food prep work. I don't know how long Max and John will be tied up."

"It's going to be a little longer than when I talked to the three of you. Jacques' assistant has accused John and Max of murdering Jacques. I need to find out why," Deputy Ormsby said.

Laura walked into the motor home and overheard the conversation. "No problem," Laura said. "After working the counter yesterday, I have a pretty good idea what needs to be done. Tell John and Max not to worry. We'll take care of everything."

CHAPTER NINE

After the sheriff arrived at the crime scene he personally interviewed John and Max for two hours. Jeff stayed with them, but since neither of them knew anything about the murder, the conversation was more of the sheriff trying to get John and Max to change their story or admit to something about which they had no knowledge. Finally, he said, "All right, you can go back to work at your food truck. Obviously there will be an investigation, and I'm sure we'll be talking again. I'm expecting my crime scene investigators to be here momentarily to dust Jacques' motor home for fingerprints. Oh, one other thing. Don't go out of town." With that warning he stood up and walked out the door.

"I can't believe it," John said. "I have the feeling he thinks one of us or both of us did it. You're the lawman, Jeff. Sound right?"

"John, think about it. You were accused of murder by Jacques' assistant. Of course he had to interrogate both of you, and I'm sure he'll do it again. I do think it's kind of strange that Jacques and his assistant had separate motor homes. That's a big expense. Wonder why they didn't want to share one. What do you know about the assistant, this guy named Ned Billings?"

"Not much. I understand he and Jacques go way back and at one time both of them were pretty heavy into drugs. Ned went into rehab because his wife threatened to leave him if he didn't clean up his act.

Evidently he got pretty involved in Narcotics Anonymous and goes to group meetings almost daily. Of course that's just hearsay. We worked in the same restaurant for a while, but since then I've only talked to the guy a couple of times."

"You mentioned there were rumors that Jacques had been in rehab but now was probably back on drugs. It seems strange to me that Ned would work with Jacques if he was back on drugs."

"I don't know," John said. "I'm just telling you what I've heard over the years. They have a history, and Jacques was a pretty well-known chef several years ago when he had his television show. Maybe Ned felt it was better for his career to stay with Jacques, no matter what he was doing."

"Well, back to the sheriff. I just wish you hadn't been quite so vocal about your dislike for Jacques, and you too, Max. This isn't helping your situation, and it will probably put you at the top of the sheriff's list of suspects."

"It may not help the situation, but neither Max nor I killed Jacques. Come on, Jeff, you saw how tired I was last night, and you were with me until we all went to bed."

"What I'm going to say isn't going to make you happy, but keep in mind this is what I do for a living – solve cases like this. The bottom line is that we were with you, we went to bed, but none of the four of us know what you did after we left your motor home. Do I think either one of you is responsible for Jacques' murder? Absolutely not. I'm simply thinking like the sheriff is probably thinking, and you need to be aware of it so you can protect yourself. What we need to do is find out who murdered Jacques so both of your names can be cleared. Do you understand what I'm saying? This is pretty serious, guys."

"Yes, Jeff, I understand exactly what you're saying, but right now I need to get ready for a hungry crowd that will probably be even bigger than yesterday given the fact that a murder took place in our general area. Come on Max. We'll deal with this later."

"Okay. Time to get to work," Jeff said. "The others have been doing prep work. Give us our marching orders, and we'll get through today."

*****

A few minutes later the three of them walked over to The Red Pony and were greeted by Marty. "John, I'm so glad you're here. Laura and I've done about as much as we can do without you telling us what you need. I told her yesterday I'd handle the counter for at least half the day. Les took care of the outside set-up, and it's ready to go."

John looked in the refrigerator, cupboard, and drawers and said, "Les, Jeff, let me make a list of what I'm going to want you to get from the motor homes. I stashed a lot of food in them, and I'm going to need it. After you've cleaned out the motor homes I need you to go over to the little house next to the ranch house. The owner told us we could use it to store extra food. Take the food that's got my name on it. I wrote it on the packages with a black marking pen when we got here, and put the packages in the little house so we could easily get them when they were needed. Please get over there as quickly as you can. We really don't have much time."

The remaining hours of the morning flew by, and promptly at noon the line in front of The Red Pony began to form. Around three in the afternoon the crowds thinned a little, and Marty asked Laura if she'd fill in for her while she took a break. She sat down at one of the outdoor tables and was joined a few moments later by Jeff who looked perplexed.

"Why the frown?" Marty asked.

"I can't put my finger on it, but there is definitely something off at the French Food Obsession. When they opened the line was longer than yesterday, but now it's dwindled to a trickle. The blond that's Jeb's daughter, Brianna, was one of the first ones in line. I saw her leave without any food, and she didn't look happy. As a matter of fact, a lot of the people who were some of the first to stand in line left without getting anything. That strikes me as really odd."

"Tell you what," Marty said. "We never did get the breakfast I promised to make, and I'm hungry. Since I was the one who stood in line over there yesterday, maybe I can find out something. The line is pretty short right now, so I should be back in a few minutes."

Marty walked over to the French Food Obsession food truck and stood in line. The woman at the head of the line gave her order to Ned. Marty couldn't hear what she ordered, but evidently they were either out of it or she decided she didn't want it, because she turned around and walked away with no food. As she was leaving Marty overheard her say to someone standing in line behind Marty, "Forget it, Stacie, no more specials. The chef was murdered last night, and that's the end of that. We'll have to go somewhere else." Marty noticed three other people who were standing in line walk away when they overheard what she said.

When it was Marty's turn, she said, "I'd like a piece of the quiche Lorraine." Ned peered at her and said, "Aren't you with The Red Pony?"

"Yes, I'm helping John. I decided to take a break."

"I'm surprised he's still here. Thought he'd be in the local jail by now charged with the murder of Jacques," he said as he handed her a plate with the quiche on it. Several of the customers standing in line behind Marty were intently following the conversation. "Yeah, I sure wouldn't want to eat at The Red Pony, since the guy who runs it is the person who killed Jacques," Ned said in a raised voice, clearly wanting as many people as possible to hear him.

"John had nothing to do with his murder, and you'll regret you ever accused him of it," Marty said angrily as she turned away from the food truck window.

"Well, you can tell him for me that I know he killed Jacques, because Jacques was a far better chef than that little pipsqueak will ever be. It was a pure and simple case of jealousy, only Jacques was murdered because of it."

Marty ignored him and carried her plate back to the table where Jeff was waiting for her. "Marty, I couldn't help but overhear Ned. If it turns out that John didn't kill Jacques, John can sue Ned for slander. I think that was pretty stupid on his part to say what he just said to you."

"Jeff, I won't even acknowledge you said 'if it turns out John didn't kill him'. There is no way John killed him. For Pete's sake, he carries spiders he finds in his bathtub outside and turns them loose, because he doesn't believe in killing any living thing, even a spider. We need to find out who did this. My purse is in the Pony, and I have a pen and writing pad in it. Let's start thinking what we can do to help John by making a list of possible suspects. I'll be back in a minute."

"I had a bite of that quiche while you were inside," he said a few minutes later. "It's really pretty good."

"Guess I ordered the right thing," she said as she sat down. "Okay, we have Jeb Rhodes and his daughter Brianna..." She was interrupted by the ringing of Jeff's cell phone. He made a motion to her indicating he was going behind the truck to take the call because of the noise coming from the nearby sound stages. He returned a few moments later and said, "I'm going to have to call the sheriff. I just got some information he needs to know about."

CHAPTER TEN

As Jeff reached for his phone and started to call the sheriff, Marty put her hand on the phone and asked, "What was that call about?"

"I didn't want to alarm any of you, but yesterday when all of you were busy I stood in line at the French Food Obsession and ordered the French shepherd's pie, because I kept hearing people order it and at the same time use the word special, so I decided to do the same. Neither Ned or Jacques was working the counter. If they had been, they might have recognized me, but the woman who was working the counter was so busy filling orders she never really looked at me. Anyway, I received a plate with the shepherd's pie on it. The woman told me it would be $25.00 for the special. I said it was listed for $7.95 on the board. She replied that I'd asked for the special. I thought it was very strange, but I was curious, so I paid the $25.00. When I looked down at the plate I saw something on it that was barely visible. I almost missed it because the thing was wrapped in tin foil, and the tin color of the pie plate almost matched it perfectly. Naturally, I wondered what was in it. I unwrapped it, and I was pretty sure I recognized what it was."

"You certainly have my curiosity aroused. What was it?" Marty asked.

"It was a capsule, kind of like a vitamin pill. I thought it was a drug that is referred to on the street as a molly, so I called one of my men at the Palm Springs station and asked him to drive out here, get the capsule from me, and have the department test it. The results just came in, and I was right, it is a molly."

Marty sat back in her chair and stared at Jeff for a moment. "This is unbelievable. I guess the operative word was when the customer used the word 'special.' It must mean that when you used that word you got the drug, and because I didn't ask for the special yesterday, I didn't get the drug served to me. Now let me tell you what happened just a couple of minutes ago while I was standing in line waiting to order." She told Jeff about the young woman standing at the head of the line and what she said to several other people who were in line.

"Jeff, do you think Jacques was selling mollies?"

"Given the fact there was such a price difference between the special and the regular and that difference is about the cost to buy a molly on the street, I would say it's a definite possibility."

"Go ahead and call the sheriff, then let's talk about this some more."

Jeff walked over and stood next to the fence while he called the sheriff. A few minutes later he returned. "The sheriff is sending one of his deputies to my office to pick up the capsule as evidence. He said this complicates the murder case even further, because now there's a drug angle."

"I don't know if having illegal drugs involved is relevant to helping us catch the killer, but the evidence sure is pointing that way," Marty said. "What I can't figure out is how Jacques made any money. He had to spend a lot of money to buy the mollies."

"Marty, like I said, the difference in the regular price of the meal and the price of the special is just about what a molly goes for on the street. Yes, if he was selling them, and it sure looks that way, he was making money."

"Okay, I agree, but he had to buy them from someone. There must have been a dealer involved."

"Yes, that's true," Jeff said, "but remember last night when Laura overheard raised voices behind the French Food Obsession talking about money? I wonder if it was the drug dealer either coming for money or giving Jacques the drugs."

"I don't know, but here's another angle," Marty said. "You saw Brianna standing in line this morning as soon as the French Food Obsession opened, and then you said she walked away without getting anything. Maybe she was getting mollies yesterday from Jacques. It certainly fits with you seeing her at the food truck a couple of times and what I heard her father saying to her. I wonder how long people feel the effects from a molly."

"Depends on the strength, but usually about three to four hours. I probably saw her over at the truck three times. She also might have been buying for a friend as well as herself. I wasn't paying attention to how many times other people were there. She's just such a beauty, that I couldn't help but notice her."

"Jeff, I told you before she's young enough to be your daughter."

"Marty, I was simply doing what nearly every red-blooded American man does. I was admiring a beautiful woman."

"Like I said, she's young enough to be your daughter. Okay back to the murder. Here's a stretch, but there's another possible suspect we might want to think about, Brianna's father, Jeb Rhodes. Certainly he hated the fact that his daughter was dropping mollies. I think that's the term I heard him use, anyway, did he hate it enough to kill Jacques or hire someone to kill him? And don't forget I overheard him make a phone call to someone called Sid and tell him 'I've got a job for you to do tonight.'"

"Aren't you making a big leap by assuming that Brianna told her father she was getting the drugs from Jacques? It's pretty unusual for a drug user to voluntarily tell someone who their supplier is, particularly if that someone just happens to be your father."

"I don't know. Another thing I'm curious about is why someone like Ned, who supposedly is so active in Narcotics Anonymous, would continue to work in a place where the owner was selling drugs. That doesn't make a lot of sense to me."

"Sweetheart, there are a lot of things in this world that don't make sense."

"There's one more person, Jeff. Don't forget about Jacques' ex-wife. I wonder if she knew he was selling drugs. If she did, maybe she thought he was making a lot of money from it, but at the same time he was still stiffing her on the child support."

"Another conundrum. Let's wind this up. We need to get back and help John and Max."

"I agree. Give me a minute to recap. We have the following possible suspects," she said as she looked at her list. "Jeb Rhodes, Jacques' ex-wife, and the dealer who supplied Jacques with the drugs, plus I'm still not certain about Ned. Maybe he secretly hated Jacques for selling drugs. Maybe he should be a suspect."

"Maybe, and don't forget about John and Max. Just because you know them and like them doesn't necessarily mean they should be left off of your list."

Marty glared at Jeff. "They are definitely not on my list of suspects."

"May not be on yours, Marty, but I can guarantee you they're on the sheriff's."

CHAPTER ELEVEN

Marty felt like she was two people for the rest of the afternoon and evening. One Marty was busy taking orders, collecting the money due for the orders, and serving people their food. It was twice as busy as the day before, because the French Food Obsession had lost a lot of their business and customers were going to The Red Pony instead. It was pretty evident that the young music festival attendees weren't all that interested in pricey French food. The other Marty was trying to make sense of everything she'd learned in the last twenty-four hours. Finally, at nine that night she told John that since she hadn't been able to talk to Jeb Rhodes last night, she'd like to try again tonight. Laura agreed to fill in for her.

She walked over to the restroom and repaired as best she could the damage from working in the heat all afternoon. It was very quiet at the ranch house when she walked up to the porch. She rang the doorbell, and it was opened a few moments later by a younger version of Brianna who Marty estimated to be about twelve years old.

"Hi," Marty said. "I'm wondering if Jeb Rhodes is here. My name's Marty Morgan, and he called me a few days ago and left a message about having me appraise his California Impressionist art collection."

"Sure. I'll go get him. Why don't you come in out of the heat? I'll be back in a minute."

Marty looked around at the paintings displayed in the large western style living room. Her immediate thought was that whoever had decorated the room had done a superb job. The paintings hanging on the walls blended perfectly with the western and Native American artifacts displayed in glass cases. She felt her pulse quicken as it always did when she was in the presence of really good art and antiques, and there was no question in her mind that these were really good.

The large man she'd seen the night before walked into the room. Last night she'd only observed him from a distance, and she realized she'd missed the easy grin and laugh lines around his eyes. *He may have problems with his daughter,* she thought, *but he's obviously been able to enjoy life as well.*

"Mrs. Morgan, I must say I'm very surprised to see you here at this time of night. What brings you to my neck of the woods?" he said as he put out his hand and shook hers. "Please, come over here and let's sit down. I'm sipping on an iced tea. May I get you some or perhaps something stronger?"

"No, thank you, I can only stay a few minutes. I wanted to apologize for not returning your call, but I was finishing up an appraisal and then a good friend of mine asked me to help him with his food truck here at the festival, so that's why I'm here at such an unusual hour. I hope it's all right that I came here this late."

"Yes, I'm glad you did. I understand there was a little excitement this morning at the food truck court. As a matter of fact, I was there. It seems that one of the owners of a food truck was murdered. This is not the kind of thing the producer of a festival such as this one wants to hear. We get enough bad publicity from kids who either drink too much or avail themselves of illegal substances."

"Actually, I'm well aware of the murder. My friend's food truck is next door to the French Food Obsession, and our motor home is next to the one where the man was murdered. My statement was taken today by the sheriff, but I didn't observe anything, so there wasn't much for me to say."

"Strange place for a murder. I feel there must be more to it than a random act of violence."

"I agree, but I don't know what the motive could be. I'd not met the man who was murdered until yesterday," Marty said.

"One of my employees interviews all the vendors and does a background check on each of them. He'd heard that Jacques Rushon had become one of the shining stars in the chef world here in the Palm Springs area and then became involved in drugs. Gene told me that Jacques had spent some time in rehab and was trying to turn his life around. That's why he decided to take a chance on him. Given the turn of events, I'm not so sure that was a wise move. Anyway, let me give you a quick walkthrough of my collection, and then I'd be interested in hearing what you think of it."

Although Marty had planned on spending only a few minutes at the ranch house, she couldn't disappoint Jeb who clearly loved his collection. "You can see that I've specialized in the California plein air painters of the early 20th century," he said, gesturing to the paintings by some of the best artists of the period.

"Mr. Rhodes, I don't need to tell you about the caliber of your collection. It's incredible. To see works by William Wendt, Guy Rose, and Edgar Payne in one collection is very rare. I would be honored to appraise your collection. Have you had it appraised in the past? And what's the purpose of the appraisal?"

He was quiet for a few moments, looking down at his hands. After a long pause, he evidently came to some inner decision, and he began to talk, "Mrs. Morgan, I feel I can trust you. The collection was appraised many years ago, because my insurance company insisted that it be if they were going to insure it."

"Yes, that's very common. I do a lot of appraisals for an insurance company for just that reason," Marty responded.

"Well, this will be a little different. You just met my daughter, Gigi. She's the one who answered the door. I have another daughter,

Brianna." He stopped talking and slowly took a sip of the iced tea next to him as he appeared to be carefully contemplating what he was going to say next. "Brianna has been a challenge to me. Her mother died a few years ago, and I've had to be both a mother and a father to my girls. I've done fine with Gigi. Brianna, not so good."

"I'm sorry. I've never had children, but I know they can be challenging."

"That might possibly be the understatement of the year. You see Brianna is a beauty and plenty of people, men in particular, will do anything for a beautiful woman. In Brianna's case, it's developed into a little drug habit, no, make that a pretty big drug habit. I've tried everything short of putting her into a rehab facility, but that's probably going to be the next step. I've convinced myself it's for her own good, and I believe it."

Instinctively Marty put her hand on his arm. "I'm sorry, this must be so difficult for you, but I'm still unclear as to what type of an appraisal you need from me, and please, the name is Marty."

"And you can call me Jeb," he said smiling. "Marty, I'm worried that if something happens to me Brianna will sell my collection for whatever she can get in a quick sale and use the money from the sale to buy drugs. I don't know whether or not rehab will work, but I need to set up a separate trust for Gigi. If something happens to me, I don't want her to be penniless because of her sister's drug habit. What I need from you is an appraisal based on the fair market value for my paintings, in other words a value that Gigi could realistically expect to get in the future if she needed the money. My attorney would set this up as a trust which is separate from my main trust and manage it until Gigi is of a legal age. As it stands now, if anything were to happen to me, both girls would inherit equally and knowing Brianna, there's a good chance she would spend all of her money and then start working on Gigi's."

"I'm certainly not a lawyer, but won't there be quite a few years before Gigi can inherit anything, since she's not of age?"

"Yes, but the age I have in my present trust is eighteen, which is not that far away for Gigi, and the paintings are simply lumped in as part of my overall general estate. As I said, I want to set up a separate trust fund for the benefit of Gigi with the value of my paintings funding that trust. Do you think you can do an appraisal of that type?" Jeb asked.

"Of course, but I have a suggestion. You haven't said anything about the rest of the things in this room, and I'm assuming you have other valuable pieces in the rest of the house as well. From what I've seen, you have some superb western and Native American artifacts. What if I drew up two appraisals? I could do one that focused only on the paintings and another one that encompassed the rest of the items. That way, you'd have a very clear idea of what the value is of the assets you want to place in a special trust for the benefit of Gigi. And Jeb, don't give up on Brianna. A lot of people turn their lives around, and she very well might be one."

"Thanks, Marty. That sounds like a good plan. Why don't we walk through the house, and you can get a sense of what I have here? Once you see what I have, I'd like you to draw up a proposal of the time you'd need to spend on the appraisals and the amount you'd charge me for preparing them."

"I'd be happy to. I really need to get back and help my friend at the food truck, so I'll do a very quick walk-through if that's all right with you."

"Absolutely, let's get started."

A half hour later Marty said, "I'll get back to you within a few days with a proposal. I'd really enjoy doing the appraisals. You have a wonderful eye for collecting beautiful art objects. If you don't mind, I'd like to ask you something. Your house is decorated so tastefully, and you mentioned your wife was deceased. I'm wondering if you'd mind giving me the name of your decorator? My clients are often anxious to find a decorator who's able to incorporate their art and antiques into a comfortable setting."

Jeb smiled and said, "You're looking at the decorator. I've done all of it myself. It's kind of a hobby of mine."

"My compliments to you. You certainly have mastered your hobby."

"Marty, while we were walking through the house, I kept thinking about the man that was murdered who owned the French Food Obsession food truck. I've had one of my employees follow Brianna for some time trying to figure out where she's getting her drugs. He told me she made several trips to that food truck yesterday, and when she came home last night, she was clearly under the influence of an illegal drug called a molly.

"A few minutes before you arrived I received a call from my employee. He said Brianna had gone back to the French Food Obsession as soon as the gates opened today, but she didn't buy anything and never went back the rest of the day. Putting two and two together, I wonder if the man who was murdered was selling drugs from the truck, and since he was dead the drugs were no longer available. Do you know anything about that?"

I sure do, but I promised Jeff I wouldn't say anything.

"Jeb, I wish I could help you, but I honestly don't know, however there is one thing that makes me think your theory might be correct. The crowds at the food truck were very large yesterday. Today they were down considerably, and your theory could be the reason. My fiancé is a detective with the Palm Springs Police Department and is also working with me as a volunteer helper at the food truck called The Red Pony. As you well know, your property is under the jurisdiction of the county sheriff, but my fiancé will be helping him. I'll tell him about your suspicions."

"Thanks. If there's anything I can do so other parents don't have to go through the agony that I'm going through, I'd be happy to help. I'll look forward to hearing from you," he said as he opened the door for her.

"Good night, Jeb, and again, I'm sorry about your problems with Brianna."

I always wanted children, she thought, *but maybe I've been spared the pain of seeing a child in trouble.*

CHAPTER TWELVE

When Marty returned to The Red Pony she saw there was a long line snaking away from it. She hurried in, grabbed an apron, and said, "My turn, Laura. I'll finish up. Sorry, I really didn't plan on spending that much time at the ranch house."

"Marty, is everything okay?" Jeff asked. "I was about ready to go to the ranch house and see if you were all right."

"Yes, I'm fine. I had a long talk with Jeb Rhodes, and I'll tell you all about it later. Right now it looks like we have a lot of hungry people, almost kind of like a feeding frenzy. What caused it?"

"Several of the sound stage venues are setting up for the next set of bands, so there's a short break in the action. I think it's also a case of people needing food to absorb the drugs and booze they've ingested. Looks like a lot of those cups are holding Fireball cinnamon whiskey, rather than soft drinks."

"I've never heard of it. What is it?"

"It's a type of whiskey that's the big thing with the younger generation drinkers. The people who make it did a brilliant job of marketing it, and I'm told it's pretty much the drink of choice at music festivals."

"I'm so out of it. This is a whole new world to me," Marty said. "I've never heard of any of the bands, a molly, or Fireball whiskey. I've decided I must be a complete nerd, and if you want to call the wedding off, Jeff, I'd understand."

"Marty, I'd be more inclined to call it off if you did know what those things were. I've got to get back out there. It's the time of night when people drop even more napkins and plates than ever on the ground. I can't tell you how much stuff I've picked up today trying to keep the area around The Red Pony clean. Oh, by the way, the sheriff was here a little while ago. He's coming back when the Pony closes at midnight."

"What does he want?"

"He wants to talk to John and Max again, and quite frankly, that's a cause for concern. I just wish John hadn't been so vocal about his dislike for Jacques. The sheriff told me he'd talked to quite a few people around the streets where The Red Pony is usually located at lunchtime and where Jacques also set up his truck. Several people apparently told the sheriff that John felt Jacques was horning in on the Pony's popularity, and John was quite open about his intense dislike for Jacques. I guess a few of them also said Max didn't like Jacques at all. See you in a little while. I'm off to clean-up duty."

The rest of the night went by in a haze of taking orders, filling orders, and counting money. Marty was certain that in the short time she'd been back to work she'd taken in several thousand dollars. The line was so long John had asked Les to stand beside her and open up another line, so they wouldn't lose any business. It was a madhouse of people, music, and a sweet pungent smell that Les said came from marijuana. As Marty served her last customer, an announcement came over the festival loudspeaker that the gates were closing in five minutes, and all attendees needed to leave the area.

*****

"I know I speak for all of us when I say I can't remember ever being this tired. I hope John feels the money he's making this weekend is worth it," Laura said as she gratefully accepted a glass of wine from Les.

"He had to have made a lot of money today. It kind of makes me nervous that he's keeping it in the motor home. I'd feel better if we could get to a bank, but since it's Saturday night and tomorrow's Sunday, guess that's not going to happen," Jeff said.

"Actually, I remember him telling me he had a safe built into the floor of The Red Pony, and I imagine that's where he's put the cash," Marty said. "Pretty smart thinking on his part, plus I've noticed there's a lot of security here, and with the gates closed I think his money is just as safe here as it would be anywhere."

"Good, that's one thing I don't need to worry about," Jeff said. "I sure would like to know exactly what the sheriff is saying to John and Max about now. When he talked to them this morning, their answers were pretty straightforward. Maybe one of them threatened Jacques during lunchtime in Palm Springs, and he heard about it."

"Well, I'm sure they'll be over here as soon as the sheriff leaves. I don't envy them being interrogated as tired as they must be. At least we got some breaks today, but the two of them never took a break from noon to midnight. That's got to be exhausting."

Jeff turned to Marty and said, "Tell me about your visit to the ranch house. Is his collection worth appraising?"

"Absolutely. It's one of the best I've ever seen. What was really interesting is what he told me about his daughter, you know, the one who's young enough to be your daughter," she said laughing with a twinkle in her eye. She spent the next few minutes telling him what Jeb had told her about Brianna's drug abuse problems.

"That certainly fits in with everything we were talking about earlier," Jeff said. He turned to Les and Laura. "Let me fill you in on what I was given at Jacques' truck yesterday when I ordered a special." He summarized what he'd been given at the French Food Obsession and about the molly capsule as well as his suspicions of why the lines had been so long there yesterday and why they had dwindled to a mere trickle today. "What you found out from your talk with Jeb at the ranch house coincides with my thoughts that Jacques was selling the mollies out of the food truck and referring to them as a special."

"From what you're telling us, Jeff, that definitely seems to be what was happening and while it explains a lot, it still doesn't tell us who murdered Jacques, and it doesn't help John or Max," Laura said.

"That's true. I'd like to spend all my time helping John and Max find out who murdered Jacques, but I've got to get back to work. There are a number of cases I'm working on, and I was pushing it with my captain when I took yesterday off. What about you, Marty? You had pretty good luck helping to solve a couple of other murder cases. Do you have some time you can spend trying to solve this case?"

"I'm between appraisals at the moment, so yes, I have a little free time. Jeb didn't seem in a particular hurry for me to do his appraisal, so I could spend a couple of days seeing what I can find out. I'm just not sure where to look."

Laura looked over at her. "I'm still getting a feeling, actually a very intense feeling, that it has something to do with the food truck. I have no idea why I'm saying this, but I think you need to talk to Jacques' wife and to Ned's wife. If the two men have been longtime friends, maybe one of the wives knows something. It's just a hunch I have."

"I'll take your hunches over anyone else's, Laura," Marty said. "Jeff, you have ties at the police station. Could you get me addresses and phone numbers for both of them?"

"Sure, but I'll need to know their names, although it should be pretty easy to get Ned's address. By the way Laura, what makes you assume that Ned's married?"

"In addition to getting psychic feelings about things, I'm pretty good at noticing things. For instance, when Ned was accusing John and Max this morning of murdering Jacques, I noticed he was wearing a wedding ring. I don't know why, I just did, and it stuck with me. I'm certain he's married. Tell you what Marty, I was planning on taking the first of the week off, so why don't I help you? I'd like to meet both women. Often I can pick up a little something extra about someone when I'm talking to them."

"That would be great. We'll start with Ned's wife and try and figure out a way to find out who Jacques' ex-wife is and where she lives. Any thoughts about how we can do that, detective?" she asked, grinning at Jeff.

"Yes. I just had a thought while Laura was talking. Since it's an ex-wife, that means he's divorced. That also means some sort of legal action took place. I'll have my secretary search the local divorce court records first thing Monday morning as well as try to find out where Ned lives. Shouldn't be too difficult."

"Before we go charging off to interview these two women I think we need to ask ourselves if we're missing anything? In other words, could someone else other than the ones we've talked about be the killer?" Les asked.

"Of course it's possible," Jeff said. "It could be nothing more than a random act. The parking lot is open to everyone who has a parking pass, so it could have been anyone. We talked briefly about a drug dealer, but I'm not sure how we could identify, much less, find that person. It could also be someone from Jacques' past that we know nothing about, however, we in law enforcement always start with who has the most to gain when someone is murdered."

"Well, that would pretty much eliminate his ex-wife, because if he's dead there is definitely no way he could pay his back child support," Marty said.

"I agree, but I still think you should talk to her. At one point in time she was his wife, and she may know if someone had a grudge against Jacques."

"That's true, Jeff, and she'd also probably know a lot about his drug use. Maybe the dealer who sold him the molly capsules is the same one he bought from when he was married to her."

"With Jacques dead Brianna wouldn't have that source to buy from, but from what Jeb told me, she got her drugs from multiple sources. I really don't think he's anything more than a concerned father, and even though he has a motive, I just don't see him doing it."

"He didn't," Laura said with certainty. The others turned to her and she continued, "We need to talk to the wives. One of them knows something, and we need to find out what it is. I'm getting a strong psychic feeling about this. Trust me, I know I'm right."

Just as she finished talking there was a knock on the door, and John and Max walked in. The expression on their faces clearly indicated they were badly shaken after their conversations with the sheriff.

CHAPTER THIRTEEN

"Come on in and sit down," Les said to John and Max. 'I imagine you'd like something to drink. I've got wine and beer," Les said.

"I'll take a beer, and I know Max would like one too, right?" he said turning to Max who nodded.

"Well, what did the sheriff have to say? Were you able to convince him that you two didn't do it?" Marty asked.

"We tried, but I have a feeling he doesn't believe us, or he thinks we're hiding something from him," John answered.

"Why do you say that?" Jeff asked.

"He told us he didn't have enough evidence to arrest either one of us right now, but that he certainly wasn't ruling it out. He said he learned from several people today that I'd talked about how I hoped something bad would happen to Jacques and how much I disliked him."

"I know you've told us the same thing several times, but I assumed you told us because we're your good friends," Laura said. "I've talked to you before about toning down your speech. You have a tendency to pop off with whatever's on your mind. Do you think people would testify that you wanted Jacques dead?"

"Yeah, unfortunately I do."

"Boss, you was jes' sayin' what a lot of people think about him. Shoot, I said the same thing a bunch of times too," Max said.

"I know, and I think that's why we both could be in big trouble. I honestly think he's going to arrest us after the festival ends. Jeff, you're the lawman. What do you think?"

"We've been talking about it while you were being interviewed by the sheriff, and we've come up with a couple of ideas we're hoping will lead to finding out who the murderer is. What really concerns me is this. I was telling Les, Marty, and Laura that the first thing the police, or in this case, the sheriff looks at when investigating a murder is who has the most to gain. Unfortunately, you have a lot to gain with Jacques being dead. From what you've told us, he had become your major competitor. With him gone, The Red Pony is still the number one food truck in Palm Springs."

"I never thought of it that way, but now I can see why the sheriff considers me a suspect, but I don't understand why he thinks Max is a suspect too."

"John, it's not the least bit uncommon for two people to plot a murder, and certainly employees are oftentimes in cahoots with their bosses when it comes to committing a criminal act. I want to know what you can tell me about both Jacques' and Ned's drug use. Who knows? That could possibly be a reason why Jacques was killed," Jeff said.

"I told you pretty much everything I know. I learned about Jacques when he had his television show and rumor has it he was let go because of his drug use. He wasn't around for several years, and I've always assumed the rumors about him going into rehab and then seclusion were true. One day several months ago I looked out the window of The Red Pony at lunchtime and there, pulling in next to my truck, was Jacques in his food truck, the French Food Obsession. Since then he's pretty much been wherever I've been at lunchtime. I have five different locations I go to, a different one each day during the work week, and you have to admit the odds of him just popping up on the specific street where I'm parked are pretty low. I know he was trying to cash in on my success, and I really resented it. All that's true, but I didn't resent him enough to murder him."

"Did you ever have any reason to think he'd started doing drugs again?" Jeff asked.

"Boss, I can answer that. I seen him give some guy money once and the guy gave him a small bag of something. The guy was real seedy lookin'. I 'member thinkin' at the time that I was seein' a drug deal go down."

"Max, how long ago was that?" Jeff asked.

"It was 'bout two months ago."

"What can either one of you tell me about Ned Billings, his assistant?" Jeff asked. "I think you mentioned that he and Jacques were friends from a long time ago, and that Ned was pretty active in Narcotics Anonymous. Anything else?"

"Yeah. I actually worked with Ned a few years ago," John said. "It was just before he quit doing drugs. I remember his wife came to the restaurant where we were working and in front of everyone told him she was going to leave him if he didn't stop doing drugs right then and there. She said he hadn't been home in several days, and she didn't know what else to do. Poor Rita was crying and carrying on something awful. I felt sorry for her, but it must have worked because he took a week off and when he came back to work, he was like a different man. He told me once that NA saved his life and his marriage."

"So Rita Billings is his wife? Do you know if he's still married to her?"

"I'm sure he is. I never heard he'd gotten a divorce."

"One more thing, then I think both of you need to get some

sleep. If tomorrow is anything like today, it should be a madhouse, plus I've heard that Sundays are the busiest days at these festivals."

"Shoot, Jeff. What's the one more thing?" John asked.

"Why and how did Ned start working for Jacques in the food truck?"

"That I don't know. Ned bounced around at a number of restaurants in the Palms Spring area, most of which were actually pretty good. When I worked with him I found him to be quite talented. All I can think of is that he and Jacques remained good friends, and when Jacques opened up his food truck he probably asked Ned to be his assistant. He was with Jacques from the time Jacques first opened it up. That's about all I know.

"I'm beat guys, and I'm sure Max is too. I'm planning on being at the Pony about ten tomorrow morning. I could use some help from Les and Jeff in the morning to help me transfer the last of the food in the motor homes over to the Pony. You got everything out of that building the owner let us use, right?"

"Yes, we transferred everything and brought it here. Are you going to have enough food?" Les asked.

"Yeah, it's going to be close, but I think we'll be okay. Worst case scenario is we just close down early. As jammed in as these motor homes are, I can't imagine trying to maneuver one out and then get it back in if we needed to make a run and buy more food. No, we'll be fine. Let's call it a night, Max. You ready to go?"

"Boss, I'm so tired I'll be lucky to get in bed before I pass out, and that durned sheriff sure ain't helpin' my stress level." The two of them stood up and slowly shuffled out the door.

"Jeff, I think we're all about as tired as they are, but I have a question, and I'll bet everyone else does too," Marty said. "Why didn't you tell them about the molly capsules, and that we're pretty sure Jacques was selling drugs out of the French Food Obsession."

"It was a very deliberate omission on my part and here's why. First of all, the sheriff has told them they are considered suspects. If they don't know about the drugs, they can't say anything to him about them. Having them even mention drugs could be another red flag for them.

"The second reason is the sheriff would know that their knowledge about the drugs being sold at Jacques' food truck came from me. Professionally, that would be a problem. The sheriff could call my captain down at the Palm Springs station and complain, and I might say with good cause. I'd be furious if someone in law enforcement told potential suspects about something that had been discovered concerning an ongoing investigation in which I was involved. And to play the devil's advocate, what if John and/or Max did it? I know none of us wants to even entertain that possibility, but it's like the four-thousand-pound elephant in the room. It has to be addressed."

"Neither one of them did it. I know that," Laura said. "I've got a strong psychic feeling about the two of them, and it's saying they did not do it."

"Laura, I believe you and I feel the same way, but I can practically guarantee you that the sheriff would laugh you out of his office if you went in and told him how you felt. He might be rolling on the floor in laughter when you went on to tell him that the reason you know they didn't do it is because you're a psychic. I've seen your psychic gift work first-hand, but the sheriff hasn't, and if he's anything like most people, at best he'd regard your claim with a great deal of skepticism."

"Unfortunately, I'm sure you're right," Laura said, "which is all the more reason for us to help find out who murdered Jacques. Let's get through tomorrow, and then we can concentrate on solving the crime and removing the cloud of suspicion surrounding our friends John and Max. See you all in the morning." All four of them quickly got in their beds and were sound asleep almost immediately.

CHAPTER FOURTEEN

Promptly at ten the next morning, everyone met at The Red Pony. The festival was scheduled to be open from noon to six on the last day, so Laura, Marty, Les, and Jeff agreed they would split their time manning the counter, three hours each, and if the crowds weren't as big as they expected they could reduce the two lines to one line. Laura and Marty, along with John and Max, helped prep the food for the day. Jeff and Les brought the remaining food from the two motor homes, set up the outside tables, and generally did whatever John asked. By 11:45 they were ready to go and promptly at noon the crowd once again came surging through the entrance gate.

The next six hours flew by. Even with two lines, customers still had long waits. The reputation of the Pony's excellent food had evidently gotten around by word of mouth. It was another huge monetary day for John and The Red Pony. The only thing that cast a shadow on the day was the overlying cloud of what the future held for the Pony, John, and Max.

At six that evening, the last of the revelers left the festival, having had an experience they knew they'd never forget. John looked at his group of volunteer helpers and said, "I don't know how I can ever thank you. When I decided to see if I could get the festival promoters to accept the Pony as one of the food trucks, I honestly had no idea it would be as hectic as it turned out to be or as profitable as it was. Let's get outta here. Why don't all of us go to the compound so you can unpack your things from the motor home while I start prepping for tomorrow's lunch and clean up the Pony. After you've unpacked, Les and Max can return the motor homes and Laura, if you wouldn't mind, you can follow them in your car and then bring them back to the compound. Jeff, since your car's at the compound, you can go on home if you want. Does that work for everybody?"

"John, that sounds fine. I need to go to Lucy's and pick up Duke. She's probably tired of putting on his pink booties, so he'll go outside on the grass to do his business," Marty said, thinking about her dog's bizarre habit of refusing to walk on the desert floor or grass without his pink booties firmly in place. The fact that he was a large black Labrador retriever wearing hot pink booties made it almost comical. Marty thought it had gone way past the amusing stage, but it didn't look like his behavior was going to change in the near future, so she was resolved to simply accepting the dog's behavior for what it was, stranger than strange.

"Fine with me. I do need to get home and use my computer to check on the status of a couple of cases I'm working on," Jeff said.

After they returned to the compound and unpacked the motor homes, Les and Max left to return them to the rental agency. Jeff turned to Marty and said, "Well, sweetheart, this weekend at the Desert Country Music Festival was quite an adventure. If I hadn't met you and you hadn't introduced me to your sister and her group, I never would have had that experience. I'll check on getting the information for Rita Billings and Jacques' ex-wife. I'll call you when I know something." He put his arms around her and kissed her. "You know, our wedding's getting closer, and after that I'll be living here permanently. It can't come too soon for me."

"Me neither, Jeff, but the thought did occur to me that if John's arrested for murder, he won't be able to do the catering for the wedding reception which was going to be his gift to us."

"I know. That thought occurred to me as well. Just another reason for us to figure out who the real killer is. We'll make it happen. I know we will."

"Glad you're so confident. I'm feeling less and less so."

"Marty, I feel that way about every case. It's kind of like climbing up a mountain. At first it seems insurmountable, but with each step you get closer to the top. Eventually you can see the other side, and you know you've made it. We're getting closer to the top of the mountain. I feel it."

"Okay, Detective Combs. I'm going to just have to take your word for it and believe me, I hope you're right."

He gently released her and walked out to his car. "If you don't believe me, ask your sister. Bet she'd agree with me." He blew her a kiss, got in his car, and drove away.

Marty walked back into her house and called Lucy. "Hi, Lucy. I just got back from the music festival. Okay if I come by and pick up Duke? You're probably getting tired of putting those booties on him, anyway."

"Honey, I think he's gonna be real happy to see ya', but I gotta tell ya', ain't never seen 'nuthin like that dog and his booties. The old man and I laughed so hard the first time we put 'em on him we had tears rollin' down our cheeks. I gotta tell ya', it's a sight to behold. Sure, come on over. Don't think I'll tell him. He'd probably get too excited."

"Great, I'll be there shortly."

When Marty drove into Lucy's driveway, the first thing she saw in the front fenced yard was Duke in his pink booties. When he saw her car he started running around in circles, going so fast that the pink booties on his feet and his black fur blended into an indistinguishable blur. In the background she saw Lucy bent over with laughter. She got out of the car and let herself in the yard.

"Duke, come," Marty said. The big black dog ran over to her and laid down on his back indicating he wanted a tummy scratch. She gave him one and then walked over to Lucy, Duke by her side, whimpering with excitement at seeing her. Marty had met Lucy when she'd first moved to High Desert to live in the four-house compound owned by her sister, Laura. Lucy was in charge of the photo department at the Hi-Lo Drug Store and the one who developed the photos Marty included in her appraisals. As different as they were, a friendship had been formed, and Marty thoroughly enjoyed Lucy's warmth and simplicity.

"Lucy, I can't thank you enough for taking care of Duke. You were right about the festival. It was definitely not a place for dogs. Between the loud music, people, and non-stop noise it would have been a nightmare for him, to say nothing of the unbearable heat. I hope he behaved himself."

"Other than refusin' to go outside without his booties, he was a perfect gentleman. Made my old man and me think maybe we need to get a dog. I had one when I was a kid, but I ain't had none since. My ex didn't like 'em, so I got outta the habit of havin' one. Need to rethink that a bit. Ya' know how I always look up a thought for the day? Well today I decided I would jes' take the first thing I saw when the computer landed on the site I use. Guess what it said?"

"I have no idea, but given what we're talking about, I assume it has something to do with dogs."

"Yep. Said the time had come for me to share my love. Guessin' it means I should share my love with a dog. My ol' man and me've been jawin' 'bout it all day. Gonna check out some sites."

"Are you looking for a certain breed?"

"Ain't thought ahead that far. Guess we'll know when we see one we like. Think we'll go to the county shelter. Be willin' to bet there's one in there that would like to be adopted. See, ya' done gone and changed my life by lettin' me keep ol' Duke over the weekend," she said grinning.

"Hope you say the same thing after you've had a dog for a while," Marty said laughing.

"I put Duke's things on the porch here. Bet yer' tired and jes' wanna get home and go to bed. I hear them music festivals are somethin' else. I guess there's a lot of drugs, booze, and who knows what else."

"Don't know about the what else, but yes, I can tell you drugs and alcohol were alive and well at the festival. I don't see how those people can do it for three days in a row. Maybe it's an age thing."

"I coulda' done a three-day booze thing when I was younger, but I can't even drink no more than a couple of beers now. And drugs? Nah, weren't never my thing. Actually, purty glad it weren't!"

"You're right, I am tired and ready to get in bed. Again, thanks. I'm between appraisals, but I have one coming up in a week or so with some of the best California paintings I've ever seen. Think you'll enjoy the photos. See you soon," Marty said as she opened the gate for Duke. A few minutes later she was on her way back to the compound.

When Marty opened the gate, Duke happily pranced in, enjoying the attention of the other residents who were sitting at the picnic table in the courtyard. "Marty, here's the last of the food from the festival," John said. "I know you're probably tired of looking at it, but as exhausted as all of us are, we couldn't even consider cooking something. Help yourself, and then we can all go to bed for some much deserved sleep."

CHAPTER FIFTEEN

The next morning Marty's ringing cell phone woke her up. She looked at the monitor and saw it was Jeff. "Good morning, Jeff. I hope you slept as well as I did last night. I feel rested, but in spite of a good night's sleep, I think I'm going to be tired for several days."

"Believe me, I slept great. I ate a tuna sandwich while I was standing at the kitchen sink, put the plate in the dishwasher, walked in to my bedroom, and collapsed. I think it was all of 7:30. I did manage to wake up early, so I decided to go to the station and see if I could find Rita Billing's address for you. Fortunately, it was really easy. Got a pencil and a piece of paper?"

"Give me a moment. Okay, shoot." She listened and wrote down the address he gave her. "Jeff, I'm not sure what I should say when I go to her home and start asking questions. I know yesterday we talked about Laura and I both going to see her, but in retrospect, I don't think that's a good idea. She might find two women calling on her and asking questions very intimidating. I could say something like I was working with law enforcement on the Jacques Ruchon case and wondered if she could tell me anything that would help me track down the murderer. What do you think of that?"

"I think it's probably a good idea if Laura doesn't go with you for that very reason, although selfishly I'd like to see someone else go with you for protection. A murder has been committed, and we don't know who did it. For all we know it could have been Ned's wife. Do me a favor and take your gun with you. Don't say anything. I know what you're thinking, but I've been involved in this game a lot longer than you have, and strange things happen when there's been a murder. Just humor me, okay?"

"All right, but I really don't like to carry a gun in my purse."

"In this case, I don't care whether you like it or not. It could save your life, so please just learn to like it. I really do want to be married to you, and if you're a corpse, that won't be possible."

"That's a cheery thought," Marty said. "Thanks."

"You're welcome. When do you plan on visiting Mrs. Billings?"

"I was thinking I'd go over there around noon. I'm assuming Ned will continue to use the French Food Obsession truck to feed people at lunch time, however a thought just occurred to me. Did you learn from the sheriff if Jacques had a Will? I wonder what the legal status of the truck is right now? Since Jacques has a child and evidently he's not currently married, does that mean the child will inherit the truck, and if so, would it be sold?"

"I don't know. Good question, Marty, but like you, I imagine Ned will be selling lunch today, and while he's gone it would be a good time to go over to his house. Another thing to consider is we don't know what the business arrangement was between Jacques and Ned. Ned may be a part-owner of the truck and there might be an agreement that if something happened to one or the other of them, the survivor would own the truck. As a matter of fact, there's a lot we don't know. Guess time will tell."

"I hadn't even thought of that. I simply assumed Ned went ahead with the food at the festival because it was already scheduled, but if he opens the truck for business today, he might be the last man standing so to speak, or the full owner of the truck."

"I'll call the sheriff and see if he's found out anything new on the case. I'll make a special point to ask him about the business relationship between the two of them and if a Will has been found. I'm sure they must have searched Jacques' home by now. Maybe they found one there. I've got another call I have to take. When you get through with your meeting, I'd like to hear what happened."

"Will do. I love you. Talk to you later," Marty said as she ended the call.

She got out of bed, put on her robe, and motioned for Duke to follow her, pink booties in hand. When she was coming back from walking Duke she saw that the door to Laura's house was open. "Laura, it's me. Okay if I come in? I need to talk to you for a minute."

She heard Laura's voice coming from the far end of her small home. "Sure, I'm back in the bedroom. Come on in."

Marty and Duke walked down the short hall and she said, "Laura, I've been thinking it might defeat our purpose of calling on Rita Billings if both us are there. She might feel intimidated. I think it would be better if I went by myself."

"Great minds think alike or something like that. Couldn't agree more. I woke up this morning and thought the same thing."

"You said you can often tell certain things about a person by talking to them. What should I look for?" Marty asked.

"There are some basic body language things that will tell you a lot. Some of the common signs of lying are talking really fast, rapidly changing body positions, or talking too much. A couple of others are if a person stares at you without blinking or won't look you in the eye. Another one is when a person crosses their arms over their chest. That indicates they may feel vulnerable or they're rejecting what you're saying. Those are the biggies. Just make a mental note of anything she does that you might consider to be the slightest bit out of the ordinary."

"Okay, I can do that. I've never thought much about the subtleties of body language, but I guess from what you're saying there's a lot to it."

"It's huge, and I think what makes it so interesting and relevant is people do these things subconsciously. They may be saying one thing, but their body language indicates something entirely different. Do you want me to watch Duke while you're gone? I'll be here all day."

"Thanks. That would be great. Jeff called and gave me Rita Billings' address. Evidently they live in an older part of downtown Palm Springs. I'm curious about her. She must really love her husband to put up with his years of drug abuse. Don't think I could do it."

"Fortunately, I don't think you'll have to, what with Jeff being as opposed to drugs as he is."

"Yes, that's a blessing in today's world. Particularly after what all of us saw this weekend. I need to stop by John's. I've got a question for him. I'll fill you in when I get back this afternoon. I'm leaving around 11:30."

Marty knocked on John's door and said, "John, it's Marty. Okay if I come in?" She knew he was usually cooking in the morning preparing for the lunch crowd who'd be waiting for The Red Pony to show up.

"Sure, Marty, the door's open, come on in."

She saw him bent over the kitchen counter cutting out dough. "What are you doing? That looks interesting."

"I'm making mini pizzas. I buy the refrigerated pizza dough and use a round cookie cutter, spread a little pizza sauce on each one, and top them with a bunch of different things. Some people like to buy a plate of them and others just like a couple. I've found them to be really popular, and they're so easy to fix."

Max was standing nearby, stirring a big pot on the stove. "What's in the pot, Max? Sure smells good."

"Got a big batch of chili in here. It's weird, but the weather turned kinda cold and really windy last night. Don't happen very often this time of year, but it's desert cold out there now. Anyway, when I got here this mornin' I talked the boss into lettin' me make chili and cornbread and servin' it at the Pony today. When those people leave their offices for lunch, and it's blustery cold, they're gonna be real happy to have a steamin' hot bowl of chili they can chow down and it'll make their tummies warm."

"You sleep as well as we did last night?" John asked.

"It may go down as one of the best night's sleep I've ever had. John, I can see you're really busy, but I have a question for you if you don't mind. Do you have any idea what the business arrangement was between Jacques and Ned? Particularly in regard to the food truck? And lastly, do you expect it will be parked today where it's been parked the last few months at lunch time?"

John looked up from cutting his mini-pizzas. "Interesting questions. I'll answer the last one first. I'd be willing to bet my first born, if I had one, that Ned will be there. He and Jacques have done well taking my overflow and when the lines are long at the Pony, I've noticed that people tend to eat at their truck rather than taking the time to go into a restaurant, order, and wait for their food.

As far as the status of their business relationship, the only thing I know is once I heard Ned call Jacques his partner. I remember it because I thought at the time it was interesting because as arrogant as Jacques was I was surprised he'd even have a partner. Ned specifically said, 'Hey partner, you need to get back here. There's a call for you on your cell phone. Want me to get it?' That's all I know about their business relationship. As far as the truck goes, the thought occurred to me this morning that if they were partners, Ned probably would get the truck. Does that help?"

I don't know. I was just curious. Thanks a lot and good luck today. See you this evening. Oh, one more thing. Are you serving something tonight that I should think about all day?" Marty asked, laughing. Long before she'd moved into the compound, John had lived there and generally prepared the evening meals for the compound residents in exchange for a modest monthly payment they each made to him to pay for the food. He kept telling them that since they served as his tasters for new dishes, he shouldn't be paid for the meals, but all of them felt more comfortable compensating him for the amount of time he spent on their meals. It was a win-win situation for everyone.

"If you like the smell of the chili, you'll probably like dinner. I told Max to make a bigger batch than usual and keep plenty here for dinner tonight. He also made an extra batch of honey cornbread. I think you'll be happy."

"Trust me, I'm already happy," she said as she walked out the door.

CHAPTER SIXTEEN

Much as she hated to, Marty went to the locked desk drawer where she kept her small pistol and put it in her purse. She took Duke out for a commune with nature and then she looked on Google maps for the location of the address Jeff had given her for Rita Billings.

Downtown Palm Springs was about a thirty-minute drive from the compound. The residents of the compound all liked the quiet solitude of living in a rural area away from Palm Springs which oftentimes provided a second home for the wealthy and a place where the snowbirds gathered in the winter. The wealthy homeowners of the city were the main reason Marty's appraisal business had done so well in the short time she'd lived in the area. Wealthy people tended to surround themselves with things of value and insurance companies often required appraisals before they would insure them, all of which was a very good thing for Marty.

She waved to John and Max as they pulled out of the driveway in the Pony. A half hour later she found the address Jeff had given her and parked her car at the curb in front of the house. When she looked at the house her first thought was it reminded her of a woman who had been beautiful when she was younger but hadn't aged well at all. The lawn was nothing but dried grass. Withered flowers peeked out of pots next to the front door whose blue coat of paint was peeling. The shutters next to the windows needed to be remounted, and the driveway was filled with holes and cracks. Lonely weeds had sprung to life in them. She couldn't help but wonder about the people who lived in the house, based on its exterior.

Marty walked up to the front door and rang the doorbell which had pulled loose from its frame and was hanging on a thin wire next to the front door. The door was open and through the screen Marty could see flickering figures on a television screen. A few moments later a woman came to the door and said, "What can I do for you?"

"I'm looking for Rita Billings. Are you Rita?"

"Maybe I am, and maybe I'm not. Why do you want to know?"

"As you're probably aware, Jacques Ruchon was recently murdered. Although I'm not with the sheriff's department, I'm helping some law enforcement personnel get information about him. We know your husband was working with him. If you have a minute, I'd like to talk to you."

The woman was clearly hesitant to let Marty in, but finally she said, "I'm Rita. I don't think there's anything I can tell you about Jacques, but come on in. I can't talk too long. I'm a hairdresser, and I have several clients coming to the shop this afternoon. I just came home for lunch."

Marty walked in and said, "Thanks. I appreciate this. I won't keep you long. I was wondering if your husband and Jacques were partners?"

"Yeah. Ned fronted the money for the food truck when Jacques asked Ned to work for him. Jacques didn't have the money for the French Food Obsession. Jacques was the front man, because he'd been a big deal chef with a television show at one point, but between drugs and child support, he was busted. Ned thought the French food truck idea was a good one, and it's turned out to be pretty successful."

"So with Jacques' death, your husband will be the sole owner of the French Food Obsession truck."

"That's what Ned tells me."

"Mrs. Billings, do you have any idea who might have killed Jacques."

She paused for a moment and looked away from Marty. Marty remembered what her sister had told her about people who wouldn't make eye contact. She wondered if what she was going to say next was a lie.

"I have no idea, but you might want to start with whoever Jacques was getting his drugs from."

"I'm sorry," Marty said, "I don't know what you mean."

"Nothing, I didn't mean anything," Rita said.

"I've heard Jacques used to do drugs. I also heard he was fired from his television show because of it. Is there any truth to that?"

"Yes."

"Did you know him well?" Marty asked. She was interrupted by the ringing of Rita's cell phone.

"Excuse me," Rita said, "This won't take long." Rita walked into the hall and even though she was speaking quietly into the phone, Marty was able to overhear what she said. When Rita returned she said, "I'm sorry, but I needed to take that call. Now where were we?"

"I asked you if you knew Jacques well."

"Let me answer, and then I really do need to get back to work. Jacques, Ned, and I used to do drugs together at night after Jacques and Ned were through cooking at whatever restaurant where they were working. That's how they met. They became very good friends. I became pregnant and lost the baby because of my drug use during the pregnancy. The drugs caused me to have extremely high blood pressure which resulted in the baby being stillborn when I was 8 ½

74

months pregnant. I was devastated. I made a vow to join Narcotics Anonymous and get clean, which I did. I haven't done drugs since then. I eventually got both Jacques and Ned to join as well. It's not a pretty story, but at least that part of our life is over.

"Ned is very faithful about attending NA meetings. He goes almost daily. That was his sponsor on the phone, and he was curious why Ned hadn't been to the regular meetings this weekend. I told him about the festival and that Ned would be returning to the meetings today or tomorrow." She stood up indicating it was time for Marty to leave.

"Rita, if you think of something that could be relevant to the case, I'd really appreciate it if you'd call me. Here's my phone number." While Marty was writing it down her eyes slid over to the phone Rita had put on the kitchen counter, and she saw the name of the person that had called Rita, Chuck Weston, displayed on the phone.

Laura was right. Rita lied to me. I know she lied to me about the phone call because I could hear her end of it and she never said Ned was at the food festival, but what she did say was pretty strange. I'll have to see if Jeff can make sense of it when he comes for dinner tonight.

Marty thanked Rita again for her time and walked out to her car. She looked at her watch and decided she had time to stop by her friend Carl Mitchell's antique shop. He always had a number of California Impressionist paintings for sale and with the Jeb Rhodes appraisal coming up in the next week or so, it would give her a head start on her valuations.

A few minutes later she walked into the shop and saw Carl finishing up a sale with a customer. He smiled at her and said, "Be with you in a minute Marty. Take a look around."

"That's why I'm here. Don't hurry on my account." She spent the next few minutes examining the California Impressionist paintings hanging on one of the walls in the antique shop. As she looked at them she decided that while they were very good, the ones hanging in Jeb Rhodes' ranch house were better.

"So Marty, what brings you in today? Involved in another appraisal that just happens to have a murder attached to it?" he asked laughing. Carl had helped her on a couple of occasions when her appraisals had also been a very important part of solving a murder case. Every time he saw her he commented on the appraisal he'd helped her with when Laura had used her psychic powers along with a knife to slice open a wig stand and find a missing diamond ring.

"Yes and no. I'm going to be doing an appraisal of California Impressionist paintings along with some other Western and Native American objects, and I wanted to get a leg up, so to speak, by seeing what you had. You've got some really good ones on display."

"I've kind of developed a reputation for that type of art and you know how it is, people talk. When someone wants to sell a piece of that type of art, they come to me, and by the same token, when they want to buy that type, they come to me."

"After I do the appraisal, I'll bring in lunch one day in return for you looking at photos of the pieces and giving me your opinion."

"Happy to do it, Marty, but with your eye I don't think it's necessary."

"It may not be necessary, but I'd feel better if you did." A thought occurred to her, and she continued, "Carl, didn't you tell me once that your brother had been greatly helped by the support he got from Narcotics Anonymous?"

"Yes, but I fail to see what that has to do with Impressionist paintings. Am I missing something?"

"No. It has absolutely nothing to do with them," she said laughing. "I just had a conversation with a woman about the organization and how much it had helped her. I guess it made me think of your brother."

"I know what you mean. I do that all the time. I'm thinking of one thing, and it leads to another and so on and so on."

"Carl, I'd like to get in touch with a man who's in NA. Do you think your brother could help me with that?"

"I don't know. It's an organization that, like Alcoholics Anonymous, is pretty much based on anonymity, but if you have the name of someone, that's not being anonymous. What's his name?"

"The name of the man I'd like to get in touch with is Chuck Weston."

"Doesn't ring a bell with me, but that's no surprise. I'll give Pete a call tonight and see if he knows him. Mind if I ask why? You don't strike me as a person who has a drug problem."

"I don't, and I'd venture to say I'm one of the few people around who hasn't even tried pot. I gave up smoking cigarettes years ago and decided I probably had an addictive personality and would be much better off leaving drugs alone. About my only vice is having a nightly glass or two of wine. The reason I want to talk to this man is because I think he may have some knowledge about the death of a man named Jacques Ruchon. You may have heard about it."

"He was that chef that had a television show for a while, wasn't he? As I remember he was the flavor of the month chef for some time and then for several years I never heard anything more about him. Recently I remember hearing he had a French food truck that was pretty popular at lunch time, but I've never been to it."

"That's right. I'm helping some people try to solve his murder. I don't know if this is a part of it, but I have reason to believe drugs may have been involved. I'd really appreciate it if you would ask your brother to call me if he knows Chuck Weston. Actually, I'd like a little more information on the organization, so why don't you have him call me either way."

"Will do. I'll look forward to seeing those paintings. I know I've been in this business a long time, but show me a good piece of art or a well-preserved antique, and I still feel like a kid on Christmas morning. I guess that tells you a lot about my life. Actually, that's pretty pathetic, isn't it?"

"Not at all. Think of all the people who wake up every morning dreading going to work. You must be excited every day wondering what possible treasure is going to be brought to you that day."

"That's about it." Just then the bell over the front door rang as a couple walked into the store. Carl turned away from her and greeted the man and woman.

A few minutes later Marty was on her way home, looking forward to the promised chili dinner as well as discussing the day's events with Jeff.

CHAPTER SEVENTEEN

"Hi, Duke. Thanks for waiting for me," Marty said as she opened the gate and patted the very excited Labrador who waited in the same place for her every time she left the compound. Everyone knew if Duke was lying down in front of the gate with his nose under it, Marty wasn't at home. If Duke wasn't there, Marty was home. It was really quite simple!

Laura saw her walk by and opened her door. "Hey, Marty, why don't you come in and tell me how your meeting went."

"I'll tell you and Les all about it when Jeff gets here, but you certainly were right about the body language thing. At one point Rita Billings looked away from me, and I was pretty sure she was lying. Then I overheard a phone call that she didn't realize I could hear. What she told me about the call didn't match what I'd heard her say to the caller. I found out a few things, but nothing that really helps me figure out who killed Jacques. I should know more tonight."

"I'm looking forward to hearing about it. I assume you don't want John and Max to overhear the conversation, since they're out of the loop on the drug angle Jeff discovered. They're usually working in John's kitchen before dinner getting it ready, so you can tell us then."

"Yes, that's a good idea. We can talk privately then. Laura, what's wrong? You have a really funny look on your face."

"I just thought of something. If Jacques was selling the molly capsules at the French Food Obsession and certainly everything seems to indicate that he was from what you were told about Brianna, what happened to the capsules? I don't recall Jeff telling us that the sheriff found any. Of course, since Jacques was murdered in his motor home that means the food truck wasn't the scene of the crime, so maybe that's why the sheriff's department didn't search it, but I find that hard to believe. I'd think they'd investigate anything that had the slightest thing to do with Jacques, wouldn't you?"

"I sure would. When Jeff gets here I'll definitely ask him if the food truck was searched. Right now I'm going to change my clothes and write a proposal for Jeb Rhodes. I really do want to get that appraisal, and if I drag my feet, he may think I'm not interested and call in another appraiser. See you in a little while."

*****

At six that evening Marty's cell phone rang. She looked at the monitor and saw the call was from Jeff. "Hi love. I'm feeling very virtuous at the moment."

"And why would that be?" Jeff asked.

"I just sent my appraisal proposal to Jeb Rhodes. If I get it, and I think I will, not only am I be going to appraise some incredibly beautiful paintings, I'm also going to be making some good money. Oh, hold on a minute. I just got an email." She read it and yelled, "Whooppee! That was fast. He approved it and asked when I could start. That definitely makes my day. So why the call? Running late?"

"No, I'm about five minutes away and just wanted to tell you I missed you today, especially after we were together all weekend."

"That's really sweet of you, Jeff. I felt the same way, but I did find out a few things today I want to talk to you about when you get here. I'll be waiting by the gate. See you in a few." She ended the call.

"Come on, Duke. Let's go greet Jeff. I won't even put your

booties on."

They walked out to the gate just as Jeff parked his undercover car in front of the compound. He smiled as he walked up the sidewalk. "You know, pretty soon I'll be walking up this sidewalk and spending the night. Of course that's after we're married, and I make an honest woman of you." He walked through the open gate and hugged her.

"Can't happen soon enough for me, if that's any consolation," Marty said. "I saw Les and Laura having a glass of wine in the courtyard. Let's join them. John and Max are probably in the kitchen fixing dinner. I know what it is, and I think you're going to like it."

"I'll bite, literally. What's on the menu tonight?"

"Chili with all the trimmings along with honey cornbread. I don't know if there's anything else, but John told me about those two items this morning."

"Hi Laura, Les. Did you recover from the weekend?" Jeff asked as he sat down at the communal picnic table located in the center of the courtyard and poured a glass of wine for himself and Marty.

"I can speak for both of us, Jeff," Laura said. "It's a good thing we didn't have one of our California earthquakes last night, because I don't think any of us would have even felt it. We were totally exhausted and would have slept right through it even if The Big One hit last night. And you?"

"I told Marty this morning I made a tuna sandwich, ate it standing next to the kitchen sink, and collapsed in bed at 7:30." He turned to Marty. "By the way, my secretary was able to get an address for Jacques' ex-wife and also some background information. Her name is Jennifer Ruchon. She works at The Golden Truffle restaurant in downtown Palm Springs. She's a cocktail waitress there. They've been divorced for five years, and there was one child from the marriage, a boy named Adam who's fourteen now. Jacques owed her several thousand dollars in back child support when he died. She and her son live in an apartment. Here's the address."

"That's great, Jeff. Thanks. I'll pay her a visit tomorrow. Okay, I need to tell all of you what I found out today." Marty recounted her visit to the Billings home and her conversation with Rita. "Here's what I think is the interesting part. She got a call from a man named Chuck Weston who, according to her, is Ned's Narcotics Anonymous sponsor. What I found interesting is she reassured him in their phone conversation several times that she was fine. She said Ned was worried because he thought she'd been working too hard. She also said that he, meaning Chuck, didn't need to worry any more about Ned working with Jacques, because she'd made sure that was no longer a problem."

"What do you suppose she meant by that?" Laura asked.

"I have no idea, but she lied to me about her phone conversation and said that Ned's sponsor was worried because Ned hadn't been to any NA meetings over the weekend. She said that she'd told Ned's sponsor that Ned had been working in the food truck at the festival all weekend and that was the reason, why he hadn't attended any meetings. Definitely not what I heard her say. What do you make of that?"

"I sure wish I could talk to his sponsor, although it probably wouldn't do any good. People who are in a twelve step program take their anonymity pretty seriously," Jeff said.

"I stopped by my friend Carl's antique shop to look at his paintings, since I knew I'd probably be appraising similar ones when I do the appraisal for Jeb Rhodes," Marty said. "While I was talking to Carl, I remembered him telling me once that his brother credited Narcotics Anonymous with turning his life around, and as a result he was quite active in NA. I asked Carl if he could find out from his brother if he knew a man by the name of Chuck Weston. Then I asked him to have his brother call me either way. I'm hoping to hear from him tonight."

"I'll run Chuck Weston's name through our police database and see what I can find out about him," Jeff said. "If he turned his life around he may have had some brushes with the law."

"Good idea," Laura said. "By the way, Jeff, do you know if the sheriff searched Jacques' food truck and if so, did he find any molly capsules there?"

"I'm sorry, I guess I didn't tell you that his men did search the truck and they found nothing. That's why my molly capsule became so critical, because it's the only thing that directly connects illegal drugs to Jacques."

"You're the lawman here," Les said. "What do you think happened to the molly capsules. Why weren't they found in the truck? Were they in the motor home with Jacques? Had he taken them there when he locked the food truck up for the night?"

"The only thing that was found in his motor home was some cocaine. Evidently that was what he'd been addicted to before he got off drugs, and it would make sense if he'd started using drugs again that he'd go back to the one he'd used before."

Laura sat quietly turning the stem of her wine glass. "I know you all would like to get some nice solid things from me, but that's not how this gift or curse I have works. I feel that Ned's responsible for getting rid of the molly capsules. Think about it. If he has stayed off drugs, and from what we know, he has, and he's also very active in NA, he would probably be very opposed to drugs. So what happens when his closest friend and from what we've heard, his partner, becomes addicted once again? How do you think he'd feel about molly capsules being sold out of a food truck of which he's a part owner?"

She continued, "I thought from the beginning of this weekend that it was strange Ned and Jacques would each have their own motor home rather than share one. Maybe Jacques wanted to do drugs, actually he probably did do them, and he knew Ned would be opposed. Maybe he felt guilty about doing them around Ned. Maybe he needed to sell the molly capsules to pay for his own habit, and maybe, just maybe, Ned killed him to save himself from the temptation of once again becoming addicted to drugs. Maybe Ned was afraid he was losing his own resolve never to take drugs again.

Maybe Ned thought it was wrong to sell them to the young festival goers. I don't know, but I sure am getting feelings that some of this might be right. Thoughts?"

All of them remained quiet for a few minutes as they thought about what Laura had just said, and then they heard John's voice. "Give us ten more minutes, and dinner will be ready."

"Laura, I think everything you said has some merit to it. I don't know whether or not we'll ever know if Jacques' return to drugs was proving to be too much of a temptation for Ned. The only person who could tell us that would be Ned, and I rather doubt he's going to talk about it. As to whether he's the killer, it's certainly something to think about."

"Jeff, do you know if the sheriff considers him to be a suspect?" Marty asked.

"No. From the sense I got after talking with him is John and Max seem to be the two main suspects. If it were my case, I'd spend some time with Jacques' ex-wife, Jennifer. We know they had an argument that day, but like we've said before, if Jacques is dead, he can't pay the back child support he owes her. So it's sort of a never-ending circle. She may have hated him for not paying it, but if he's dead he can never pay it."

"Well, don't forgot about the possibility that his drug dealer might have killed him because Jacques owed him money. We did hear loud voices arguing the night of the murder."

"That's true, but I can also tell you that trying to find a drug dealer is like looking for a needle in a haystack," Jeff said.

At that moment John and Max walked out of John's kitchen carrying a large kettle of chili and some individual soup bowls. They made several trips back and forth and when they were finished, chili, bowls of grated cheese, chopped onions, red pepper flakes, cornbread, soft butter, and a large tossed green salad made quite a presentation on the communal picnic table. Small ornamental lights attached to the tree branches above them glittered as the sky began to turn into early evening darkness, giving the courtyard a festive air.

Les held up his wine glass and said, "I propose a toast to John and Max who never fail to amaze us with their wonderful creations, even if it probably does cause all of us to pack around a couple more pounds than we'd like. Gentlemen, thank you." They clinked their wine glasses and began to fill their bowls and plates. For a few moments it was very quiet in the courtyard, the only sounds being those of spoons and forks coming in contact with pottery and plates.

As if on cue, they all began to talk at once. "That was the best... How did you make that...Cornbread was awesome..." They laughed, and Laura said, "John, Max, there is no doubt in my mind this is the best cornbread and chili I've ever had. No wonder The Red Pony is such a success. I'm sure everyone else sitting here feels as privileged as I do to have the chefs of the Pony as their own nightly dinner chefs. Thank you from all of us."

CHAPTER EIGHTEEN

After dinner was finished they sat at the table talking of this and that. It was just small talk, and no one brought up anything about the murder of Jacques Ruchon or the fact that John and Max were still very viable suspects.

"Excuse me, everyone. I need to take this call," Marty said as she stood up and walked away from the table. They could hear her saying, "This is Marty," as she walked into her house.

"This is Pete Mitchell. My brother, Carl, said you wanted to get in touch with a man named Chuck Weston. I know him. What do you want to know?"

"I'd like to talk to him, but I don't know how to get ahold of him. Do you have his contact information?"

"I do, but it would be unethical for me to give it to you. You see, I know him through Narcotics Anonymous, and we don't share information about each other."

"Pete, I understand, and I won't ask you to breach that confidence, however I would ask you to do me a favor. Could you call Chuck and ask him to get in touch with me? Please tell him it's regarding Ned Billings, and that I'm very concerned about a situation in which Ned has become involved. You have my number. If you could do that for me, I'd really appreciate it."

"Yes, actually Chuck is my sponsor, and I've met Ned Billings."

"Is there anything you can tell me about Ned that wouldn't be a violation of the anonymity rules of NA?"

There was quiet on the other end of the phone, and then Pete said, "Quite frankly, several of us have been worried about Ned. The Palm Springs NA community is rather small, and there's been a lot of talk about him lately that has taken place both before and after our meetings. He's been working with a man who's relapsed, as we call it, and we're very concerned Ned might relapse as well. There's also some talk that he and his wife are having marital problems, and that's a very dangerous combination that can often cause someone to relapse."

"I believe the man you're referring to who worked with Ned is Jacques Ruchon. Are you aware he was murdered early Saturday morning?"

Marty heard a sharp intake of breath on the other end of the line and then Pete spoke, "No, I had no idea, and I don't think Chuck knows either. I just spoke with him, and he didn't say anything about it. As a matter of fact, he asked me if I'd seen Ned lately, and I told him no. This definitely changes the situation. I'll call him right now. Hopefully, he'll get back to you."

"I really appreciate it, Pete. Please tell him I'm very worried that Ned may be charged with murdering Jacques Ruchon. He may be able to tell me something that can help Ned."

"I will, Marty, but I'm curious about something. What is your involvement in this?"

"Good question. I was helping a friend at the country music festival where Ned's food truck was and where his partner was murdered. My friend's a suspect, and I'm doing everything I can to clear his name. Also, I don't like drugs, and if that's an aspect of the case, and it seems to be, I'd like to see the guilty party punished."

"That makes perfect sense. I'll call Chuck now. Have a nice evening."

"Again, thanks for calling me and for the information."

Shortly after she ended the call there was a knock on her door and she said, "Come in." Jeff walked into the room.

"Everything okay, Marty?" he asked.

She told him about the phone call and how the caller knew Chuck Weston personally. Just then her phone rang and she motioned to a chair, indicating Jeff should sit and wait for her to finish the call.

"This is Marty," she said to the unknown caller.

"Marty, my name is Chuck Weston. I understand you'd like to talk to me." She gave a thumbs up sign to Jeff.

"I would very much like to talk to you. Is there any chance we could meet somewhere tomorrow? I don't know where you live, but I'm planning on being in Palm Springs tomorrow around noon. Maybe we could meet in the early afternoon for a cup of coffee."

"Early afternoon would be fine with me, but since I'm retired why don't you come to my house about 1:30? There's a NA meeting I go to at noon. I sponsor several people, and they're all usually at that one. They would probably be concerned if I missed it. Here's my address. Let me give you directions. It can be tricky to find."

She wrote the directions down and said, "I can't thank you enough for calling me so quickly. I look forward to seeing you tomorrow. Again, thanks." She ended the call and turned to Jeff. "Hopefully by this time tomorrow night we'll be closer to finding out who murdered Jacques."

"Marty, you are carrying that gun in your purse we talked about, aren't you? I'm a little concerned about you going to some guy's house, and based on the fact you told Chuck you were going to be in Palm Springs tomorrow I imagine you're planning on talking to Jennifer Ruchon."

She walked over to her purse and opened it. "See, here it is. I'll keep it with me. I promise, and yes, I am going to see if I can talk to Jennifer."

"Actually, I knocked on your door to tell you I was going to have to leave. All heck broke loose at work over the weekend, and I've been given several new cases. I'm pretty much overloaded, and I need to catch up on some work tonight. Walk me out to the car?"

Whenever Jeff kissed or hugged Marty longer than Duke thought was appropriate, he growled at Jeff. When Marty discovered that Duke wouldn't go outside without his booties on, she and Jeff had started walking out to his car so they could have a little privacy. The only other place was Jeff's condo which Marty visited occasionally without Duke. They still weren't quite sure how Duke was going to react to Jeff moving permanently into Marty's home after they were married.

A few minutes later Marty returned and said, "Duke, think it's time for your booties. We need to take a little night walk, plus I've got a big day ahead of me tomorrow, and I need another good night's sleep."

CHAPTER NINETEEN

Marty spent Tuesday morning researching some of the names she'd seen on the paintings that she'd be appraising for Jeb Rhodes. Between the Internet and the books she owned on California Impressionist paintings, she felt confident of her ability to appraise them fairly.

At eleven, she got in her car and began the drive to Palm Springs. From what she'd seen on Google maps, Jennifer Ruchon lived in an apartment near the convention center and only blocks away from the Golden Truffle restaurant. The traffic in Palm Springs was heavier than usual and Marty wondered if a large convention was taking place. The closer she got to the convention center, the worse the traffic became.

Maybe I should just park in the convention center parking garage and walk to Jennifer's apartment. There is no way I'm going to be able to find a parking place with this much traffic. Think that's what I better do.

A few minutes later she locked her car and walked over to the elevator in the parking garage. Jennifer's apartment was two blocks away and due to the cold snap yesterday, it was a beautiful spring day in Palm Springs. She was grateful for the respite from the heat. Jennifer's apartment complex was identical to the apartment complex next to it. They all seemed to have that Southern California look with their dark pink paint, tiled roof, central pool area surrounded by palm trees, and Mediterranean iron grillwork. Fortunately, she reached the locked gate just as a couple walked out of the apartment building, and she was able to easily gain entrance to it.

Jennifer's unit was on the second floor towards the center. Marty knocked on the door, and a few moments later a woman's voice asked, "Who is it?"

"My name's Marty Morgan, and I'm here regarding the death of your ex-husband, Jacques Ruchon. I'd like to talk to you for a few minutes, if you have time."

The door was opened by the same beautiful brunette Marty had seen leaving the French Food Obsession truck after having an argument with Jacques Ruchon. Marty's impression of Jennifer was that her tan attested to hours spent outside, probably by the side of the complex's pool. Large brown eyes looked out from her flawless complexion.

Hmm, Marty thought, *with a tan like hers and given her age I'd think she'd have some lines on her face from the sun. I've heard that Palm Springs is one of the places in California that has an abundance of plastic surgeons. Wonder if she's had a little work done, at least that's what Laura always calls it, but since I heard her and Jacques quarreling about back child support, it's probably due to good genes. Don't think she could afford it, but I sure wish I could have a few of those genes.*

"Come in. What can I do for you?"

Marty walked into the neat apartment and noticed that the walls were covered with posters of California Impressionist paintings. There was a stack of books about different artists on the coffee table. "Jennifer, you must like California Impressionist paintings given the number of posters you have and the books on your coffee table."

"I fell in love with them many years ago when I was browsing through an antique shop in town. I don't know what there is about them that appeals to me, but obviously something does. You can tell from where I'm living that I can't afford any, but every time I look at my posters or check out a new book at the library, I'm happy. Maybe someday I'll be able be able to afford one."

"Funny you should be interested in them. I'm an art and antique appraiser, and I'm getting ready to appraise an incredible collection. Maybe there's some way I could get you in to see it, but that's not the reason I'm here. Even though I know you were divorced from Jacques Rushon, I'd like to extend my condolences. Since he was the father of your son, I'm sure this is a difficult time for you and your son."

"Not really. My son and I learned long ago that Jacques would never be the father my son deserved to have. I've been both a father and a mother to him, and fortunately he's a very good kid. Why are you here?"

"As you know, your ex-husband was recently murdered. A good friend of mine is a prime suspect, but I believe he's innocent. I'd like to find out who the killer is, so my friend's name can be cleared."

"There's a lot of people who might have murdered Jacques. The line of people who hated him is pretty long. Good luck on finding the specific person."

"What can you tell me about him that might help me?" Marty asked.

"I haven't seen much of Jacques for the last few years other than to try to collect the back child support he owed me. The last time I saw him was Friday when we argued about it at the music festival. A friend gave me her ticket so I could get in, but it didn't do me any good. Jacques told me to come back that night after midnight and he'd have some money for me then, but I was called into work even though it was my day off. Anyway, it was pretty much the same old story he always told me when I asked for the child support money he owed me. He always had some excuse or another."

"How much did he owe you?"

"A lot," Jennifer said sadly. "Several thousand dollars, but the drugs were always more important than his son's welfare. They came first other than the time when he got clean for a few years."

"Did you know who supplied him with his drugs?"

"No. It was like one of those revolving doors. I think you should put drug dealers very high on the list of your possible suspects. I remember when we were married and all the telephone calls he got from his dealers demanding money. If I answered the phone, they hung up."

"How did you meet Jacques?" Marty asked.

"When I met him he wasn't Jacques. He was Bert from a hick city in Kansas. He'd moved to Kansas City and started working as a bus boy in a good restaurant there. It was owned by a Frenchman who took Bert under his wing and taught him to be a chef. I will give Bert that. He was very good with food, really creative, and his instincts were very good. He felt he'd outgrown Kansas City, so he came to California and landed in Palm Springs. I met him when he was making the transition to Jacques. He developed a French accent, and we used to laugh about it. In those early days it was just fun, but eventually he began to believe his own press, if you know what I mean.

"I was working as a cocktail waitress, and after a few months we moved in together. He promised me that one day he'd be the owner of the best French restaurant in Palm Springs. For a while it looked like he might keep that promise. He was able to get a television show, and for the first time since I'd known him, he was making good money, but then he became quite friendly with a devil I call Mr. Cocaine. Eventually Mr. Cocaine took him over. There's a saying that a man takes a drink, then the drink takes a drink, then the drink takes the man. Substitute the words Mr. Cocaine, and that's what happened to Bert or Jacques as he was then called. He even changed his name legally."

"Were drugs the reason you divorced him?"

"Yes. My brother was an addict, and I know how they can mess a family up. I hate them. We'd gotten married by then and had our son. I stayed with Jacques for a long time, but eventually I had to leave him. I didn't want our son to be raised in a drug environment. He was already beginning to ask questions about his dad's behavior."

"I'm sorry. That must have been hard for both of you."

"Well, it sure hasn't been easy. Fortunately, I'm a good cocktail waitress, and I've been doing it for so long that I know how to get good tips. We make out okay, but that back child support sure would have made a difference in our lives. Guess I won't see any of it now," Jennifer said wistfully.

"How did you know he was back on drugs?"

"When you live with someone who's been on drugs you know the signs. When he wasn't taking drugs, he was a different person. It was kind of a Dr. Jekyll-Mr. Hyde thing. He just turned into a different person. About a year ago I recognized the signs. I was right."

"I understand that Jacques wanted to start a food truck business, but he didn't have enough money to buy one, so he went into partnership with Ned Billings."

"That's true."

"I also understand they were good friends."

"Yes. They met when they were both sous chefs in a well-known restaurant. It was about the time Jacques started getting into drugs. I always thought Ned played a big part in Jacques getting so hooked, because he and his wife were really into them then. They'd get together at night after the restaurant closed, and often Jacques wouldn't come home until the next day."

"That doesn't sound like a very fun marriage to me."

"Trust me, it was the low point of my life. Ned's wife, Rita, lost a baby because of doing drugs. After that she had something like a religious experience and stopped using drugs. She became very involved in Narcotic's Anonymous and eventually told Ned if he didn't stop using drugs, she'd leave him. She got him to join NA, and he in turn got Jacques to join. I always thought it was ironic, because Ned was responsible for Jacques really becoming addicted, and then he was responsible for Jacques getting off drugs. Why he went back to them, I'll never know."

"One last thing, and then I'll leave. What is your opinion of Ned's wife, Rita?"

Jennifer was quiet for a few moments and then said, "I always thought she was a bit off. Something just wasn't quite right with her. When she got into NA, she really got into NA. It was not uncommon for her to attend meetings three times a day. It became her "raison d'etre," her reason for living, if you know what I mean. It's all she lived for. I haven't seen her recently, but I've heard through the grapevine she's become pretty rabid about drugs and their evils. I also heard, although this is just rumor, that she was afraid Ned would go back on drugs, because he was working with Jacques. Like I said, that's just rumor, but she was never anyone I wanted to get close to."

Marty stood up and said, "Thank you for being so honest. I'm sorry for the troubles you've been through. I think you deserve a far better life, and maybe with Jacques gone, your time has come."

"Thanks. I could use a little stardust in my life. I'm getting a little long in the tooth to make this cocktail waitress thing work much longer, and since I don't have any other skills, might be time for me to look for a rich sugar daddy. If you find one, send him my way," she said laughing.

"I'll keep it in mind. Here's my business card with my phone number on it. If you think of anything that could be important to the case, I'd appreciate it if you'd call me." Marty opened the door and walked towards the stairs leading to the ground floor, all the time thinking about how the road people take often leads to a different destination than what they'd planned.

I feel sorry for her. She seems like a nice person that got tangled up with someone who wasn't right for her. I'm so glad I found Jeff. From what I've observed, in today's society, good men are somewhat rare and hard to find. I think I got very lucky.

On her way to the parking garage she saw a deli and realized she hadn't eaten anything since the chili from the night before. She walked in, ordered a sandwich and iced tea, and tried to make everything she knew about the case fit together. It didn't.

CHAPTER TWENTY

Marty left the parking structure and drove to North Palm Springs where Chuck Weston lived. She gave her name to the gate guard and entered the golf-oriented complex. As always, she had the feeling that the only thing that made this complex different from all the other similar ones was the name. In her mind they all looked exactly alike. Palm trees, tile roofs, and iron gates that led to atriums, along with retirees driving golf carts which seemed to be the requisite means of transportation in these types of complexes. You rarely saw children in the gated living quarters.

She easily drove to Chuck's home and gave him points for not having a yard that required water in the dry desert environment, but instead he had a front yard covered with small rocks and different varieties of cacti. It was appropriate for the desert.

She rang the doorbell of the well-kept house, and the door was immediately opened by man who looked to be about sixty. "Hello," he said. "You must be Marty. Please, come in. The weather's changed since yesterday, and it's beginning to warm up, so please come inside where it's nice and cool."

Marty followed him into the house and saw the golf course fairway beyond the patio which was covered with brightly colored plants. "May I get you some iced tea?" he asked.

"No thanks. I just had some with lunch."

"Let's go into the family room. It overlooks the golf course, and it's my favorite room in the house. We can talk in there. My wife's playing today, so we won't be disturbed."

"The view's wonderful. I can see why you like this room," Marty said.

"I'm an avid reader, and I spend most of my time here when I'm not playing golf. I retired several years ago, and we moved to Palm Springs to escape the cold Michigan winters. We've never regretted it. Now, how can I help you?"

"I don't know if you can. Let me tell you about some of the events of the last few days." She told him about the festival, how Jacques was murdered in his motor home, how her friends were prime suspects, and concluded by telling him about her meeting with Ned Billings' wife, Rita.

"I didn't know Jacques had been murdered. Our television set has been acting up, and I haven't gotten around to getting it fixed. There's so much gloom and doom in the news these days we decided to cancel our newspaper subscription several months ago. That's probably why I was unaware of it."

"Did you know Jacques?" Marty asked.

"Marty, I'm going to be honest with you. Obviously you know I'm a member of Narcotics Anonymous. It changed my life several years ago when I had a serious drug addiction problem. It almost cost me my wife and my family. It did cost me my job. Fortunately, I was very good at what I did and had been able to save quite a bit of money, but the word was out on the street about me, and no one would hire me. That's when I decided to retire and move here. I'd been clean for about a year. Since I've been here I've been very active in NA. I know pretty much most of the people who attend the meetings."

"I take it from what you're saying that you did know Jacques."

"Yes, I knew him. We often attended the same meetings, but I haven't seen him for quite a while."

"Did you know that he started using drugs again after being clean for several years."

"I heard that, yes."

"Chuck, I know there is anonymity among the members of NA, but I also know that if psychologists or doctors feel that someone is about to commit a crime, they have a duty to alert the appropriate officials. I think sometimes it's referred to as a higher law. Does that apply to members of NA?"

"Marty, that's something I've never encountered, but if it were me, and I felt there was a threat of someone doing harm, I would probably break the anonymity code."

"I'm asking you to do that, Chuck. I was at Rita Billings' home yesterday. When she took your call she stepped into the hallway. I overheard her end of the conversation. When she was finished talking to you, she came back into the room where I was, and then she lied to me. She said you had called to ask her why Ned hadn't attended any NA meetings over the weekend, and that she had told you he was at the music festival. She didn't say that. I overheard her say it wasn't a problem any longer, and that she'd taken care of it. Could you tell me what that was all about?"

Chuck was quiet for a long time. His hands were clasped in his lap and he rubbed his thumbs together, seemingly deep in thought. Finally, he started to speak. "Marty, I've been Ned's sponsor since he got clean. I think he's replaced his drug abuse with an addiction to NA. While I don't think any addiction is a good one, it's certainly better than the one he had."

"One of the friends of mine who's a suspect in Jacques' murder worked with Ned at one time," Marty said, "and he told me Ned was very active in NA."

"That's true. I wasn't in favor of him working with Jacques and buying the food truck. While the twelve step groups like AA or NA are very beneficial in group settings, I've seen problems arise when two ex-addicts decide to work together. Ned told me that wouldn't be a problem for him and working with Jacques in a French food truck was his ticket to really making it big in the Palm Springs restaurant business. He told me it was the chance of a lifetime. He felt that Jacques' star status as a television chef, even though the show had been several years ago, would be very beneficial to his career."

"I can see where he'd feel that way. It sounds reasonable."

"Yes, it did. A few months ago he told me he suspected that Jacques was using again. He also told me his wife, Rita, was strongly opposed to him working with Jacques, because she was afraid he would be a bad influence on Ned and that sooner or later, Ned would start using again. Ned told me they had bitter arguments about it."

"That's not hard to understand," Marty said.

"Well, it went beyond that. She started threatening Ned that if he didn't stop working with Jacques, she'd make sure one way or another that he did. Ned told me she'd started acting strangely, and he was concerned about her."

"My friend who's a suspect had worked with Ned. He'd met Rita and said she was the reason Ned had gotten off drugs," Marty said.

"She was. Rita told him she was going to leave him if he didn't get clean. It's not the first time a spouse has been responsible for someone getting off drugs, and in Ned's case it worked. The two of them were devout attendees of NA meetings. If you've heard that Ned is intense about NA, multiply it by a factor of ten, and you'll get a sense of Rita's intensity."

"I didn't know that. So, what you're telling me is that Rita threatened to do something if Ned didn't end his involvement with

Jacques," Marty said.

"Yes. That's the history of them and their involvement in NA. Rita called me last week because I'm Ned's sponsor, and she told me she was really concerned about the problem, as she called it. I became worried she was going off the deep end, if you know what I mean. She didn't sound at all rational. I didn't want to alarm Ned, so when I saw him the night before he went to the music festival I didn't say anything. I wish I had."

"Why do you say that?"

"I don't think Ned had anything to do with Jacques' murder, but I'm not so sure about Rita."

"What do you mean?"

"You said Jacques was murdered in his motor home. Do you know if there were any signs of a forcible entry?" Chuck asked.

"My fiancé is a Palm Springs police detective. He was at the festival with me. As a matter of fact, our motor home was next to Jacques', so he was one of the first people at the scene of the crime. Evidently Ned had gone to Jacques' motor home Saturday morning because Jacques hadn't met him at the French Food Obsession food truck at the agreed upon time. He was the one who discovered the body. My fiancé said nothing about forcible entry. Why do you ask?"

"Well, I'm talking off the top of my head here, but in my former life I was a private investigator for a very large law firm in Detroit. I've seen my share of things like this and whether or not there's been a forcible entry can be huge, because if there wasn't one, that means the victim knew the person and opened the door. Jacques would have opened the door for Rita."

It was Marty's turn to be quiet as she sat digesting what he was implying. "That's certainly a possibility, but it also could have been Ned himself. A friend of mine says to always look at who has the most to gain when someone is murdered. In this case, Ned had a lot to gain."

"I can't believe it was Ned. He had too much going for him to risk losing it all by killing Jacques. No, I can't accept that as a possibility."

"Chuck, if Jacques died, Ned would get the food truck all to himself. They'd been in business long enough that it had a following, probably because of Jacques' name. With Jacques gone he'd get rid of the temptation to do drugs again. In other words, he had a lot to gain."

"No, absolutely not," Chuck said rising to his feet, clearly agitated. "No, Ned would never do something like that. I sponsor a lot of people, and I've become a very good judge of character. I'm sorry, this conversation has really upset me. I think you need to leave."

"I will, but I want you to know how much I appreciate your time and your insights. And please, don't ever regret anything you told me," Marty said as she walked to the front door.

"As a matter of fact, I sincerely wish I hadn't said anything. I feel that I've betrayed a friend, and I don't like the feeling. Good day."

Marty walked to her car, sorry for the turmoil she'd caused Chuck Weston. When she got in her car, she took her phone out of her purse and called Jeff.

CHAPTER TWENTY-ONE

"Hi, Marty. To what do I owe the pleasure of this call? It's pretty rare that you ever call me when I'm at work. Is everything all right?" Jeff asked.

"Yes, everything's fine. I found out a few things concerning Jacques' murder, and I'd like to run them by you. Are you terribly tied up right now, or could you take a little time off for a cup of coffee? I'm in North Palm Springs."

"You picked the perfect time. The captain just left for the day, and I'm getting ready to do some paperwork. We've met in the coffee shop next door to the station before. How long will it take you to get here?"

"I can be there in about ten minutes. See you then."

She was driving up to the condominium guard gate when her telephone rang. She pulled over to the side of the road and answered it, not recognizing the caller's number. "This is Marty."

"Marty, it's Jeb Rhodes. I'm still planning on you doing the appraisal, but I'd like to talk to you first. Is there any chance we could meet for a drink somewhere around six this evening?"

She thought for a moment and then said, "That would be fine. I have some business in Palm Springs, so let's meet at the Golden Truffle. It's pretty centrally located and shouldn't be too busy that early in the evening."

"Great. Thanks for being so accommodating. I know exactly where it is, and I'll see you at six tonight." She ended the conversation and drove to the coffee shop to meet Jeff.

As she pulled into the coffee shop parking lot, she saw Jeff's broad back just as he was walking into the shop. A minute later she entered and walked over to the booth where he was sitting.

"Our air conditioning unit is having problems today, and I've been working in an overheated office most of the day. A glass of iced tea sounds like heaven to me. What would you like?" he asked as the young waitress walked over to their table.

"I'll have the same."

"We're going to make this really easy for you," he said smiling up at the young woman. "Two glasses of iced tea, and that will be it."

After the waitress left, he looked at Marty and said, "What's going on?"

"Jeff, I feel really unsettled. I met with Jacques' ex-wife today, and I liked her a lot. She seems like a really nice woman who fell in love with the wrong man. I kind of felt like we were kindred spirits. She had posters of California Impressionist paintings on her walls and a lot of books on the subject from the library. I thought it was rather coincidental given that I'm going to be doing that big art appraisal for Jeb Rhodes in a couple of days. By the way, he called and wants to meet me this evening at six. When you get to the compound, tell the others to go ahead and eat if I'm not back yet. I'll grab something when I get there."

"Why do you think he wants to meet with you? I thought you'd agreed on the price of your appraisal and when you were going to start."

"We did, so I have no idea why he wants to meet with me, but I'll let you know after I see him this evening. Anyway, the other meeting I had was with Ned Billings' sponsor, the one I mentioned last night whose name is Chuck Weston. He's the reason I have this unsettled feeling. Here's what he told me." She spent the next few minutes telling Jeff about her conversation with Chuck Weston.

"Yeah, I see what you mean. I think you've narrowed the list of prime suspects down to two people, however something just occurred to me while you were talking. Ned might very well have accused John and Max of murdering Jacques to shift suspicion away from him and/or Rita. Of course that doesn't tell us which one, if either of them, did it, but it sure would make sense. I'm sorry this isn't my case, because it certainly has developed some interesting twists and turns."

"Here's something else that's troubling me. Do you think I should go the sheriff with my suspicions?"

"Wouldn't do you any good," Jeff said. "I talked to him this morning, and he told me even though the murder was unsolved he always goes to the Sierra Nevada Mountains for the opening day of the trout fishing season. And guess what? Opening day is this weekend, and he's leaving tonight with a bunch of guys. Said he'd been doing it for years, and it was pretty much written in stone. He laughed when he told me about it and said even if his wife was the one who'd been murdered, he'd probably still go."

"I don't think that's very funny, and I certainly hope you never say anything like that about me."

"Don't worry, I won't. Plus, fishing has never been my thing. You're safe there."

"Something else is bothering me, Jeff, and I don't feel very good about it."

"What's that?"

"I kind of shamed Chuck into telling me about Ned and his wife, and I think he really regretted saying anything at all to me. He's very active in NA and while one doesn't take a legally enforceable oath regarding anonymity, it's a pretty sacred thing to them, and he broke it by telling me what he did. I feel badly about it, but I don't know what else I could have done."

"Don't waste your time regretting it. He's a big boy, and from what you told me he made his own decision regarding whether or not to violate the unwritten pledge of anonymity. What concerns me is he might tell Ned that he's told you. If Ned killed Jacques, or if he knew Rita killed Jacques, he might try to stop you from telling anyone."

"I think that's a stretch, anyway, I've never even talked to Ned other than ordering food from him at the French Food Obsession the first day of the music festival."

"Yeah, you're probably right. I guess we'll just have to see what the next few days bring, although I do think the case is getting close to being solved. Ned or Rita? Interesting. Of course, there's still the chance it was just a random murder, or Jacques' drug dealer was the one who killed him."

"Jeff, Chuck asked me something that I answered, but I didn't know if what I told him was in fact correct. He asked if there were any signs of forcible entry into Jacques' motor home, and I told him no. I based it on the fact that you'd never mentioned it, so I assumed there weren't any. Is that right?"

"Yes, the sheriff noticed that right away, and it's one of the reasons he has John and Max at the top of his suspect list. Jacques would have opened the door for them. Of course I imagine he would have opened it for Rita or Ned."

"Don't forget about Jacques' drug dealer. Certainly he'd open the door for him too. And probably for Jennifer, his ex-wife, although I'm pretty sure she didn't have anything to do with it."

"Tell you what," he said looking at his watch, "I have to get back to the office and get my paperwork finished. Why don't you talk to Laura and see if she's got any more thoughts about the murder?" He put some bills on the table and said, "Bye sweetheart, see you tonight."

CHAPTER TWENTY-TWO

Marty had two hours before she was to meet Jeb Rhodes. She knew she could stay in Palm Springs and kill time, but she really wanted to see what Laura had to say. She decided to drive to the compound even though she'd have to make another trip back into Palm Springs to meet Jeb. As she parked in the driveway she looked over towards the gate. As usual, there was Duke, patiently waiting for her.

Better take him for a walk before I do anything else. "Come on Duke," she said as she opened the gate. "Bootie time."

I sincerely hope at some point in time this bootie fixation of his will become a thing of the past. I bet that's why Jeff decided to live here when we're married rather than at his condo. He probably doesn't want anyone to see him walking Duke with his pink booties on. Probably thinks it would hurt his downtown image. Tough detective seen walking big black Lab who's wearing pink booties. Yeah, that might not be so cool. He'd probably be the talk of the police station. Can't really blame him for it.

When she'd finished walking Duke, Marty saw Laura sitting at the table in the courtyard working on her laptop computer. She walked over and sat down across from her. "Are you doing things that can't be interrupted, or can you spend a couple of minutes talking to me?"

"You take priority over my laptop any time. What's going on?"

Marty told her about her conversations with Jennifer, Chuck, and Jeff. When she was finished, she sat back and waited for Laura's response. After a few moments Laura said, "I'm getting a feeling you're in danger. I think you need to be very careful."

"Laura, that's not exactly what I wanted to hear. I would rather have you tell me who killed Jacques."

"I wish I could. I simply don't know, but for some reason I'm sure it wasn't his drug dealer. I'm not so sure he would have opened the motor home door for that person, knowing he owed him money. I have a strong sense it was Ned or his wife, or maybe both of them. Either way, I think you need to stay clear of them until this is over. Does Jeff know if the sheriff has found out anything more?"

"I don't think so. Jeff talked to him this morning, and the sheriff told Jeff he was going away on his annual opening day fishing trip. Nothing else was mentioned."

"Well, the good news about him leaving town is that neither John nor Max will be charged with murder while he's away. They came back here after they finished up with their lunch crowd and spent a couple of hours cooking for a cocktail party they're catering tonight. John said the hostess didn't want them to be at the party, because she wanted her guests to think she made everything herself. Can you believe that?" she said laughing. "John said dinner would be at the usual time this evening."

"Did he mention what he was fixing for dinner tonight?"

"Yes, he said it was hearty appetizers. My guess is they made more appetizers than they needed for the catering job, so we'll be having the extra ones for dinner."

"Well, whatever John makes, it's always delicious. Thanks for your words of wisdom. I need to go check my email, and then I have to go back to the Springs and meet with Jeb Rhodes. I told Jeff, but I'll tell you too. I may be late for dinner, so start without me. See you later."

*****

After driving back to Palm Springs, Marty pulled into The Golden Truffle parking lot. It was still warm in town and once again, she was glad she lived where she did. The temperature at the compound was always about ten degrees cooler.

She opened the door of the popular restaurant and saw Jeb waiting for her. He turned to the hostess and said, "We're not having dinner. We're just going into the bar for a drink." He motioned for Marty to follow him. Marty was amazed at the number of people who were in the bar this early in the evening. She remembered someone saying once that The Golden Truffle had the reputation for being the "go to" place after a round of golf. Judging from the crowd she thought a lot of people must have played golf today.

Jeb walked over to a table in the corner, somewhat removed from the crowd. "I didn't want to have to compete with the noise level coming from the people near the bar. I hope you don't mind that we're a bit farther away. What would you like to drink?" he asked.

"I'd like a glass of chardonnay wine. Thanks."

"So, did you recover from the music festival?" he asked.

"Yes, I finally got some sleep. And you, was your ranch a mess afterwards?"

"No, not really," Jeb said. "My manager hired a great crew that had everything cleaned up by noon the day after it ended. Actually, if you saw it now, you'd never know that thousands of people were on the property for three days. Back to business as usual." He paused as the cocktail waitress walked over to their table.

"Marty, it's good to see you again," the attractive waitress said. It was Jennifer Rushon.

"May I say the same. Jeb, let me introduce you to Jennifer Rushon. She's the ex-wife of the man who was murdered on your property. Jennifer, this is Jeb Rhodes, the owner of the White Stallion Ranch."

They shook hands, and Marty had the distinct feeling that an electric spark had spontaneously passed between the two of them. For a moment she didn't think either one of them even knew she was there. An idea began to form in her mind. "Actually, Jennifer, it's quite a coincidence that I'm here with Jeb, because he has one of the finest California Impressionist art collections I've ever seen, and I'm going to be appraising it very soon.

"Jeb, I was at Jennifer's apartment earlier today, and she has posters of California Impressionist paintings all over her walls. I think she's read every book on the subject she can find. You two certainly share something in common, a love of California Impressionist paintings."

"Jennifer, I know quite a bit about the subject, and I always enjoy sharing my paintings with people who enjoy them," Jeb said. "Perhaps you could come out to the ranch and see them. If you're here at this time of the evening, you probably work most evenings, so maybe you could come for lunch. I have an amazing chef who cooks for me. Why don't you give me your phone number, and I'll call you?"

Jennifer looked at him with a megawatt smile that lit up her face. "I can't think of anything I'd like more." She wrote her telephone number on a cocktail napkin and gave it to him.

"Thanks," he said, holding her hand a beat more than was necessary to retrieve the napkin. "I'll call you in the morning. Maybe we could even do it tomorrow."

"I'm free. Now, I better get your orders, or the bartender will report me. What would you like to drink?"

"We'll both have a glass of chardonnay wine," Jeb said. Jennifer wrote the order down and walked away from the table.

Well, when I said I'd see what I could do about finding her a sugar daddy, didn't think it would happen so fast, but Jeb Rhodes just might be her sugar daddy. I think I just witnessed the beginning of a blooming romance. Woohoo! Couldn't happen to two nicer people.

"Jeb, you asked me to meet you regarding the appraisal. What did you want to talk to me about?" she inquired as Jennifer returned to their table and set their wine glasses down in front of them, smiling at Jeb.

"I'll get to that in a moment, but thanks for introducing me to Jennifer. She's quite a beautiful woman, and if she's interested in California Impressionist art, that's a huge plus."

"Jeb, I don't know much about her, but all my instincts tell me she's a very good person. I think you heard that Jacques Rushon was a drug addict. Jennifer was married to him during that time, but divorced him because of his addiction. When he died he owed her a lot of money for back child support. I only bring it up because she hates drugs, and I know the trouble you've had with Brianna and drugs. It looks to me like you and Jennifer certainly have more than art in common," she said with a knowing smile.

"Thanks for telling me. Actually, that's part of why I wanted to meet with you. Brianna came home last night, or rather some people brought her home, and she was totally wasted. This morning I made the decision to put her into a drug rehabilitation facility. It kills me to do it, but it's my last resort. I don't want to lose my daughter to a drug overdose, and if I don't do something like this, there's a good chance I will. I'm taking her to a facility I've selected in a few hours. Her best friend is helping me. She's as worried about Brianna as I am," he said with a look of pain clearly etched on his face.

Marty reached across the table and put her hand on his arm. "I'm so sorry, but I think it will be for the best. I don't know what I can do to help, but if you think of something, please let me know."

"Thanks, but that's not the reason I wanted to meet with you. Well, actually it is part of the reason. I don't want Brianna or Gigi to know I'm having new trusts drawn up, and while I don't think either one of them would connect an appraisal with a new trust, I'd like you to do the appraisal while Gigi's at school. She leaves for school at 8:00 in the morning and gets home around 3:00 in the afternoon. I know it means you'll probably have to spend more days at my home then you may have scheduled, but you asked if you could do anything for me, and this is something you can do."

"Of course, that's not a problem. When would you like me to start?" Marty asked.

"I'd like you to begin Monday of next week. That will give me time to get Brianna situated and see if there are any problems with her at the facility. The facility recommended, based what I told them, that she spend two months there. It's a long time and a lot of money, but given what the alternative could be, I'll consider it money well spent."

"Yes, Monday will work fine. I'll be there shortly after eight in the morning. I was planning on spending two days with you, but with the time restrictions, I think I'll have to make it three days. Is that okay?"

"Yes, that's fine with me. I'll be curious to see what values you place on the paintings. I used to know to the penny what they were worth, or at least what comparable items were bringing at auction and in the galleries, but with the problems I've had with Brianna during the last year or so, I've sort of lost touch."

"That's my job," Marty said, looking at her watch. "Jeb, I need to go, or I'll be late for dinner. It's a long story, but we have a chef where I live, and although he's a wonderful chef, he's not very nice to be around if someone is late to one of his dinners. I told everyone to go ahead and start without me, but I think I can make it if I leave now. Thanks for the drink, and I'll see you next Monday." As she was walking to the door she noticed that Jeb had motioned for Jennifer to come over to his table.

I wonder if he wants a refill or wants to confirm lunch tomorrow. I'll be very curious to see where this leads.

CHAPTER TWENTY-THREE

When Marty returned to the compound, the residents were all sitting at the table enjoying the early spring evening. Just as she sat down to join them in the courtyard, Jeff let himself in through the gate. John and Max were at the picnic table as well.

"John, you look more relaxed than I've seen you in a long time. Something good happen today?" Marty asked after she was seated at the table.

"I agree with Marty," Jeff said. "Did you finally get some sleep or did you score some huge catering job? Of course if that was the case you'd probably be looking stressed. I know how seriously you take those gigs," he said laughing.

"You're both right. I feel the best I've felt in several days, mainly because I called the sheriff's office today to see if they'd found out anything new on the case, and when I got through to him the sheriff told me he was leaving for a few days to go on his annual fishing trip. He also told me he hadn't found out anything more that would cause him to arrest either Max or me," he said as he took a sip of his wine.

"And yes, I did get a new catering gig. The woman who hired us to prepare appetizers for her cocktail party tonight was so pleased with them she asked us to cater her husband's birthday dinner next month. She's invited two hundred guests, and it's really a big deal.

Her home is huge. There's a swimming pool, a theater, tennis courts, a putting green, and a guest house. If the guests are as wealthy as she is, and if we can pick up some business from them, I really might have to seriously think about renting a kitchen in town and hiring some staff. As you know, I've been flirting with doing just that for quite a while. Like I said, maybe it's time to get serious about it."

"That's wonderful, John," Laura said. "You mentioned earlier we were going to be the recipients of some of your appetizers tonight. I'm looking forward to seeing what you made for her."

"Let me go in and start the oven. A couple of them need to be heated. I think you'll be happy with them. We'll eat in about half an hour."

"Take your time, John. No one would dare leave without eating whatever it is you're making," Les said laughing.

An hour later after they'd consumed every last one of the appetizers, Marty said, "Those were fabulous. I really liked it that you had such a variety, and the fruit sticks were a nice touch to cleanse the palate."

"I could personally make a meal on those bacon waffle coins. Next time, just make the waffles a lot bigger, and I'll be happy," Jeff said.

"As always, my pleasure. It's great to have such an appreciative audience. Thank you."

"I'm going to have to say good night," Les said as he stood up from the table. "The painting muse has been sitting on my shoulder all day, you know that inner voice that gives you guidance once in a while, and I'd like to continue working on a painting that's been quite difficult for me. It will probably be an all-nighter, since I can finally see the painting begin to take shape. See you all tomorrow." He walked around the table and kissed Laura lightly on the cheek. They'd been seeing each other exclusively for ten years, but had never married.

Les had been married in his early twenties, and when the marriage ended, he made a vow to never get married again. Laura had made peace with the situation, and even though they hadn't gone through the ritual of marriage, they were as committed to each other as if they had.

"Les, you may have the painting muse, but I've got an inner voice that keeps telling me I should have stayed at work and completed the paperwork I was trying to finish. I think I'll go back to the office and get it done once and for all," Jeff said.

"I'll walk you out to your car," Marty said. "I'd tell Duke to stay, but there's no reason to since he won't go out there anyway."

When Marty walked back into the courtyard, the lights on the tree had been turned off, and the courtyard was quiet. Everyone had retired to their house for the night after enjoying another one of John's fabulous meals.

CHAPTER TWENTY-FOUR

Ned walked into his house and called out, "Rita, where are you? I need to talk to you."

"I'm in the den. Today was really busy at the salon, and I'm chilling out watching TV. I thought you were going to a meeting before you came home."

"I was, but I got a call from Chuck. He asked me to meet him at a coffee shop."

"What did he want?"

"He felt guilty about something he did today and decided he'd better tell me about it."

"Well, that sounds interesting. What was it?"

"A woman asked someone she knew in NA if he would call Chuck and have Chuck call her. Chuck did, and he met with this woman earlier today. She wanted to know all about me and also about you. She knew Chuck was my sponsor."

"Why would she want to know about us? That's kind of weird. Anyway, since he's in NA, I'd be surprised if he said anything to her."

"Unfortunately, he did. That's why he felt guilty. It was about Jacques' murder."

She looked at him with a strange expression on her face. "I don't understand what you're saying. What did Chuck tell her?"

"What it basically boiled down to was that he and she discussed whether or not either one of us was involved in Jacques' murder. I know I didn't murder him, but what about you? You've been angry about me working with Jacques ever since I bought the food truck, and we opened the French Food Obsession. I can't even begin to count the number of times you've told me how worried you were that I'd go back on drugs just like Jacques did. Rita, please tell me you didn't have anything to do with Jacques' murder," he said, looking intently at her.

"Ned, I can't believe we're even having this conversation and that you're asking if I was involved in his murder. Who is this woman? Why is she so interested in the case?"

"Her name is Marty Morgan. That's all I know about her. She told Chuck that a friend of hers was a suspect in the murder, and she wanted to clear his name. I've never heard of her before. She must be a friend of either John or Max. They're the only two I know that are suspects. I used to work with John a long time ago. You've met him."

"I vaguely remember him. Why are they considered suspects?"

"John owns The Red Pony. It's a food truck that's pretty popular. When we started out and before we developed a following, Jacques always parked the French Food Obsession truck as close to The Red Pony as possible, so we could get some business from people who didn't want to wait in their long lines. Even after we'd developed quite a following on our own he still always wanted to park as close to The Red Pony as possible. I know it really irritated John. I told the sheriff he was the one who killed Jacques, because John didn't want any competition from him."

"Have they arrested either of them?"

"No. So far no one has been arrested."

Rita looked Ned straight in the eye and said, "Ned, you have to believe me. I had nothing to do with Jacques' murder, but I can't say I'm sorry it happened. You know how worried I've been that you'll go back on drugs because Jacques did. With him gone you won't be around his bad influence."

"Okay, Rita, I believe you. When I was talking to Chuck I told him you would never do anything like that. I'm glad I was right. All this has me feeling pretty anxious. I think I'll go to a meeting. There's one in half an hour on the others side of town. I'll see you later. We can eat a little late tonight, and Rita, now that Jacques is gone, I think we need to work on our marriage," he said closing the front door behind him.

Although the television was on, Rita wasn't even aware of it as she frantically tried to figure out what to do. A plan began to form in her mind, a way to make sure that neither she nor Ned would ever be associated with the murder of Jacques Rushon.

CHAPTER TWENTY-FIVE

Marty spent the morning cleaning her house and emailing a client who had questions about the appraisal she'd recently sent to him. His main question dealt with the high value she'd placed on his collection. He wondered if all insurance companies charged approximately the same premium for insuring property like his or if he should shop around and see if he could get a better premium quote.

It was an appraisal that Dick, Laura's boss, had asked her to do for one of their insureds, and she felt like she was in a bind. On one hand she felt very loyal to Dick for referring the client to her, but on the other hand her actual client was the man himself, not Dick. She wrote him back and said she really didn't know the answer to the question and suggested he call several insurance companies and simply ask them what they would charge to insure his collection with the value she'd placed on it.

She was debating what to have for lunch when her phone rang. She looked at the monitor and didn't recognize the number. "This is Marty," she said.

"Hi Marty. It's Rita Billings. You asked me to call you if I thought of anything regarding Jacques Rushon's murder. Something's come up, and I'd like to talk to you. Could you meet me at my house in an hour or so?"

"Yes. Care to tell me anything about it over the phone?"

"No. I'm not sure if my calls are being monitored. I'll tell you when you get here."

"See you in an hour," Marty said and ended the call.

That's weird. I wonder what she wants. Well, maybe she can tell me something that will help John and Max. It'll take me thirty minutes to get there, so I've got time for a quick shower.

Twenty minutes later as she walked out of her house, she almost bumped into Laura. "Where are you off to?" Laura asked.

"I just got a call from Rita Billings asking me to meet her at her house. She said she has something she wants to tell me. I shouldn't be too long. If I get hung up, would you take Duke outside? My door's unlocked, and his booties are on the chair next to the door."

"Marty, don't go to Rita's. I can't tell you why, but I'm getting a strong sense that you shouldn't go. Please."

"Oh, Laura. You've said yourself that sometimes your intuition is wrong. I'm sure this is one of those times. Rita's harmless. I'll be fine and be back before you know it. Honest. Don't worry. See you later."

As she began the drive to Palm Springs, she once again thought to herself how glad she was she didn't live there. Although most people saw the city as being quite beautiful, she felt its beauty was contrived with its golf courses and planned communities. She much preferred the natural beauty of the nearby desert that surrounded the sprawling Palm Springs urban area. She loved the desert's natural landscapes and the play of color as it changed throughout the day. It seemed alive to her, while the unnatural beauty of Palm Springs seemed stagnant by comparison.

There were only a few vehicles on the streets in the run-down neighborhood where Rita lived. Marty figured everyone was at work trying as best they could to make ends meet. This was not the type of neighborhood where women stayed home, cooked evening meals for their husbands, and children played. Marty parked in front of the house she'd been to the day before yesterday and walked up to the door. Rita opened it before she could even knock or ring the doorbell. "I'm glad you're here," Rita said. "Come in."

Marty walked into the house and followed Rita into the den at the rear of the house. "Have a seat," Rita said. "I want to show you something." She walked over to the desk and opened a drawer. She took a piece of paper out of it and handed it to Marty.

Marty read the piece of paper which said "You got too nosy, and now I'm going to kill you just like I killed Jacques. You know too much to live." She looked up at Rita with a confused look on her face. "I don't understand…" She gasped as she saw the gun in Rita's hand. "What's going on?" she exclaimed in a fearful voice.

"I'm sure you don't understand, but it really doesn't matter. Chuck Weston told Ned about your visit with him yesterday. Chuck regretted telling you some of the things he did, and he wanted Ned to know that you suspected him or me of murdering Jacques Ruchon. Ned didn't kill him, I did, but Ned can never know that. I told him I didn't, and he believed me. You've learned too much, and I'm sure you'd never stop trying to dig up new evidence until you discovered I was the one who did it. I'm sure Ned would go back to using drugs if he found out. I can't let him do that. His being free from drugs is more important to me than anything else in the world," Rita said in an unnatural tone of voice, her voice rising with each word until she almost shouted the last words.

Good grief. I think she's having a mental breakdown right before my eyes. She's going to kill me. Think, Marty, think. You don't have much time.

She remembered how insistent Jeff had been that she keep her gun in her purse, but it was on the floor next to her feet. There was no way Rita would let her get to it. She did the only thing she could think of to do. She pretended she'd fainted and fell to the floor, her purse under her.

"Get up, you stupid woman! I don't have all day." Rita prodded Marty with her shoe. "Get up!" Rita reached down to pull Marty up, but as she did Marty knocked the gun out of her hand, and Rita scrambled to get it. When Rita had it in her hand she turned around and fired at Marty, the bullet hitting her in the shoulder.

At the same moment, Marty reached into her open purse, took her gun out, and fired at Rita, hitting her leg and causing Rita to fall on the floor. Just then Marty heard a voice say, "Rita, stay where you are. I've got a gun on you." Marty recognized the voice. It was Jeff's. He began to speak into his phone, "This is Detective Combs. Send two ambulances and a couple of officers to this address immediately!" He listened for a moment and said, "Murder and attempted murder." He ended the call.

Marty scooted as far away as she could from Rita and shakily tried to stand up. Instead she crumpled to the floor as she lost consciousness. Hours later she woke up in the hospital with a very worried Jeff sitting next to her bed. Laura, Les, John, and Max stood in the background with long faces.

She groggily looked at them, and tried to speak. Jeff held a cup of water to her lips, and she gratefully sipped it. After several moments she said, "Jeff, I've never been so glad to see someone in my life. How did you know I was at Rita's house? How badly am I hurt? What about Rita?"

"First things first," he said, his hand gently stroking her forehead. "You were hit in the shoulder, so fortunately none of your vital organs was hit. That's the good news. The bad news is even though the bullet only hit your shoulder, you lost a lot of blood, and you suffered a concussion. The doctor wants to monitor you here in the hospital for several days. You're going to be fine, but you need some time to heal.

"As to how I knew you were at Rita's house, well, Laura was very concerned about you, no, make that panicked. She had a hunch you were going to be in danger, so she called me at the station. I actually got to Rita's house before you did. I parked behind a delivery truck whose driver was taking a lunch break. I didn't want Rita to see me and get spooked. After I saw you walk into the house, I made my way around to the back of it. I looked in the window and saw Rita holding a gun on you. Fortunately, she'd left the sliding glass door to the kitchen unlocked, and I let myself in. That part went well. What didn't go well was I couldn't get to you in time. I don't know if I can ever forgive myself for that. I guess it's something I'll have to learn to live with."

"It wasn't your fault. You told me I'm going to be fine, so don't even think about it. I'm just glad you were there. Did you hear what she said?"

"Yes. I heard it. I also picked up the white sheet of paper she handed you, and I've already given it to the sheriff's office. One of his men called me earlier today and told me they'd gotten the results from some fingerprints they'd found in Jacques' motor home. They ran them, but there was no match. I'll bet there will be a match with hers that were on that piece of paper, plus I'm pretty sure the bullet from her gun will match the bullet that killed Jacques.

"As for Rita, she was brought to the hospital and treated in the emergency room for her leg wound. Two officers stayed with her, and when her treatment was completed, they handcuffed her and put her in the back seat of their squad car. She was taken to the sheriff's station and charged with murder and attempted murder."

"Jeff, I can't believe I fainted. I really thought I was stronger than that."

"I think I remember you telling me at the scene of another murder that you felt faint. As I recall, I told you then to put your head between your legs. This time it was a little too late for that. Blame it on the loss of blood, not nerves. Look at it this way. You solved the case. I'm sure the sheriff will be more than happy with what you did when he finds out. Congratulations."

"Thanks, but I sure don't feel so good right now. That's as close as I ever want to come to being murdered. I really didn't think I was going to make it out of there."

"Well, you did, but I have a question. Why did you pretend to faint in front of Rita?"

"I thought if I could get my body over my purse, somehow I'd be able to reach in it and get my gun. I did, but it didn't quite work out so great."

"Marty, do me a favor. In the future, why don't you stick to doing appraisals and let the law enforcement professionals do the heavy lifting?"

"I think I will, but at least John's and Max's names are clear now."

"Marty," Jeff said, "I don't think they'd feel very good if you were murdered on their behalf."

"Yeah, you're probably right, but I wasn't murdered, so all's well that ends well. Actually, I don't think I'm the first to say that. I must be feeling better. Seem to remember studying a play by Shakespeare with those words when I was in high school."

"Well, if you can remember that, I agree, you must be feeling better. It pretty much sums things up. You're going to have to give a statement sooner or later. I know these four people behind me all want to at least say hi, but the doctor told me to keep your visitors to a minimum and keep you as quiet as possible for a few days. In return you could do me a favor. If Laura asks you not to go somewhere, don't go. Could you promise me you'll do that?"

"Pretty much but not 100%. I'd like to think I have free will."

"Well, even if you don't mean it, try to say it for me. I'll feel better."

"Okay, here goes. If Laura tells me not to go somewhere, I won't, but I would like to go to sleep now."

"Good. Now I feel better," he said kissing her on the cheek as the others walked over to her and gently touched her face on their way out of the room, letting her know how much she had come to mean to all of them. "I'll be back later. Sleep, my love," he said as he closed the door to her hospital room.

CHAPTER TWENTY-SIX

Two days later Marty was released from the hospital and Jeff drove her to the compound late that afternoon. All of the residents rushed outside to greet her and tell her how happy they were that she was all right. "John," Marty said as they walked into the courtyard, "I think the worst thing about being in the hospital was having to miss your cooking. Hospital food is not my thing. What's for dinner tonight?"

"This isn't a gourmet creation of mine, but I think it's a good way to celebrate your return. We're having bacon-wrapped filet mignon steaks on bacon-flecked mashed potatoes with mushroom caps in melted butter, broccoli with hollandaise sauce, and fresh baked bread. Oh yeah, I made a little something for dessert, so save a little room," John said smiling.

"Maybe I should have someone try to murder me more often if it calls for a meal like that," Marty jokingly said as she poured herself a glass of wine.

"No, Marty, absolutely not. I think your crime solving days are over. Now that you're going to be my wife, I think I should have a little say in things like this," Jeff said with a serious look on his face.

"Okay, okay. John, I didn't want to alarm you, but when the sheriff had you and Max at the top of his list of suspects, I was a little concerned that the best chef in the Palm Springs area wasn't going to be able to keep his promise to cater our wedding reception."

"Now that this is behind us, it's time to get serious about it," John said. "How about if I make a menu for the reception, so we can go over it together and you can make any changes you like?"

"Does that include a chance to taste a few samples?" Jeff asked, laughing. "Marty, I don't know about you, but I know I'd be happy with anything John makes."

"Ditto for me, John. I think we'll just leave it in your capable hands and simply say thank you for such a wonderful wedding gift."

"Are you kidding? Because of what you did Max and I won't be cooking in a prison kitchen. We are both terribly indebted to you," he said, raising a glass as if toasting her.

"Marty, you took a big risk for the boss and me, and I'll be entirely grateful." Max said.

"Max, I think you mean eternally instead of entirely, but I'm sure Marty got the message," Laura said.

"That I did, and as I told Jeff when I was in the hospital, all's well that ends well," Marty said as she looked adoringly at Jeff and gave him a long lingering kiss. The others clapped and shouted their friendly approval of her deep affection for Jeff, her soon-to-be husband.

EPILOGUE

Six Weeks Later:

Marty and Jeff: Marty fully recovered from her gunshot wound and keeps busy with the preparations for their upcoming wedding as well as being an art and antique appraiser whose services are very much in demand. Jeff continues to be one of the most outstanding police detectives in Southern California. Several police departments in other areas of the state have asked his captain if they could pay the department to have him help them with important cases. So far Jeff has resisted, not willing to leave Marty. He knows it's only a matter of time until the captain insists he take one, as it would only enhance the department's reputation.

Laura and Les: Les finished the painting that had given him so much difficulty and sent it to a gallery who represents him in San Francisco. It immediately sold for over a hundred thousand dollars. He's working on two more paintings in the series. Laura continues to give all of the compound residents psychic guidance whenever she feels it's appropriate, and they all have learned to rely on it.

John and Max: The Red Pony's reputation continues to grow, and John made a decision to buy a second food truck. He named it The Blue Pony, and Max runs it. John also now rents space in Palm Springs and is rapidly developing his catering company, The Red and Blue Catering Service, which is growing by leaps and bounds. At

John's suggestion, Marty and Jeff decided they would be married in a private ceremony in the compound courtyard, and then they would have a "Meat and Greet the Newlyweds" barbecue reception following their wedding. Plans are underway!

Rita and Ned: Rita is in a state mental hospital following her breakdown, and it's uncertain if she'll ever be declared competent to stand trial. Her fingerprints on the note she gave Marty matched those that were found in Jacques' motor home. There was also a ballistics match. Ned's living with Chuck Weston and his wife as he struggles to stay free from drugs. He sold the French Food Obsession and in a twist of fate, is working as a sous chef at The Golden Truffle.

Lucy and Her Old Man: They're now the proud parents of a furry little baby in the form of a three month old yellow Labrador retriever. The puppy was taken to the county shelter when the owners had to move and they couldn't take the puppy with them. So far the dog is fine about going outside without booties on, but Lucy bought some just in case. She was able to find some dark blue ones and thinks they're a much better color for the dog than Duke's pink booties.

Jeb and Jennifer: Jennifer found her sugar daddy and married him within a month of their first meeting. Jeb and Jennifer are working on blending their two families together, but since her son has fallen in love with the White Stallion Ranch and Gigi is thrilled to have a mother who actually cooks and does motherly things, it looks like it won't be a problem. Brianna is doing well in rehab, so the counselors say.

Duke: He's becoming more accepting of Jeff, and there's hope he might fully accept Jeff when he begins living at the compound after the wedding.

RECIPES

WESTERN CHILI

Ingredients

1 lb. ground beef
1 lb. beef sirloin, cut into small bite-sized cubes
1 lb. hot Italian sausages
6 garlic cloves, minced
2 onions, finely chopped
2 tbsp. chili powder (if you like it hotter, feel free to add more, but if you add a lot, keep in mind that you'll need to simmer it longer to let the chili powder lose it's bitter taste and let the flavors marry)
Salt and pepper to taste
2 14 ½ oz. cans stewed tomatoes
1 14 ½ oz. can red kidney beans, drained
1 can beer
Chopped onion for garnish
Shredded cheddar cheese for garnish

Directions

Remove the casings from the Italian sausages. Place them in a 12-inch frying pan. Break them up into little pieces and fry until cooked through. Remove the sausage and transfer to a bowl. Fry the hamburger and the steak until cooked through. Remove them from the pan and put them in the same bowl. There should be some grease left in the pan after cooking the meat. Add the onion and sauté until it's soft, about 4 minutes. Add the garlic to the onion and cook for 1 minute. Remove from the frying pan and put in the bowl.

In a large heavy pot combine the tomatoes, beer, beans, meat, onion, garlic, seasonings, and stir until combined. Bring to a boil and reduce heat to simmer. Cook uncovered for one hour. (You can make this several hours in advance by cooking it to this point. If you make it in advance, put a cover on the pot. Turn off the heat and then reheat it for 30 minutes before serving.) Thirty minutes prior to serving, adjust the seasonings. If necessary, add more liquid such as beer, water, or the drained kidney bean liquid. Ladle the chili into serving bowls and garnish with the chopped onions and shredded cheese. Enjoy!

NOTE: Personally, I like to serve this with honey cornbread!

HONEY CORNBREAD

Ingredients

1 pkg. corn muffin mix (I usually use Jiffy)
1/3 cup milk
1/4 cup honey
1 egg
Soft butter

Directions

Preheat the oven to 400 degrees. Grease an 8 x 8-inch baking dish or muffin pan. You can also use paper baking cups by placing them in the muffin pan. Combine the ingredients together until just blended and then let the mixture stand for 4 minutes.

Pour the mixture into the prepared baking dish or fill the muffin cups ½ full. If using a baking dish, bake for 20-25 minutes or until the top is slightly browned. If making muffins, bake for 15-20 minutes. Serve with soft butter. Enjoy!

HACHIS PARMENTIER (FRENCH SHEPERD'S PIE)

Ingredients

2 cups chopped leftover pot roast or lamb
2 cups chopped cooked vegetables (You can pretty much use anything. I like to make it attractive to the eye, so I use a combination of colors, like orange for carrots, green broccoli, etc. You also want to use vegetables that were hardy on their own before cooking as opposed to lettuce or cabbage)
1 cup beef gravy (Unless I have some left over, I usually use a packet like Knorr's.)
2 cups mashed potatoes (Remember to use a hand potato masher as opposed to an electric mixer. It makes a big difference!)
¼ cup grated Parmesan cheese
¼ tsp. salt
¼ tsp. freshly ground pepper

Directions

Preheat oven to 350 degrees. Combine the meat, vegetables, and gravy. Season with salt and pepper to taste. Pour the mixture into individual dishes or a glass baking dish, approximately 8 x 8 inches. Spread the mashed potatoes over the mixture.

Sprinkle the top with the Parmesan cheese. If you're using a glass baking dish, bake for 45 minutes. If you're using individual dishes, bake for 30 minutes. Enjoy!

BACON WAFFLE APPETIZERS

Ingredients

10 slices bacon, fried until crisp and then crumbled
½ cup all-purpose flour
2 tbsp. sugar
2 tbsp. cornstarch
½ tsp. baking powder
½ tsp. baking soda
¼ tsp. salt
1 ½ cups buttermilk
2 tsp. vanilla extract (I use the real deal. Think it's much better than the imitation.)
1 large egg, white and yolk separated
½ cup butter, melted (Always use unsalted, because the level of salt in salted butter can really affect the outcome of a dish, and not particularly in a pleasant way.)
½ cup sour cream
¼ cup chopped chives
Waffle iron
Round 3-inch cookie cutter or water glass that has a 3-inch diameter
Mixing bowl and beaters which have been put in the freezer to chill

Directions

Preheat the waffle iron to its highest setting. In a large bowl whisk together the flour, sugar, cornstarch, baking powder, baking soda, and salt. In a smaller bowl whisk together the buttermilk, egg yolk, and vanilla extract. Place the egg white in the prepared bowl and beat until stiff peaks form.

Stir the buttermilk and egg mixture into the dry ingredients until just combined. Stir in the melted butter. Gently fold the egg white into the mixture and add the bacon bits, reserving some for garnish. Spoon 1/3 to 1/2 cup of batter onto the heated waffle iron and bake until crunchy and golden, about 2 to 3 minutes.

Remove the waffle from the waffle iron and let cool. Use your cookie cutter or glass to cut circles out of the waffles. Mix the sour cream and chives together and spread about ½ tablespoon on each one. Garnish with bacon bits and serve at room temperature. Enjoy!

MAKE IT YOUR WAY FRUIT STICKS

Ingredients

3 cups of different fruits such as strawberries, cantaloupe, honeydew melon, grapes, watermelon, pineapple, etc.
Wooden serving sticks

Directions

This is where the make it your way comes in. You can use a melon baller to make balls out of the melons. You can use cookie cutters to make stars, half-moons, or other shapes as desired, or just cut them free form. When the fruit has been cut to your liking, thread the pieces onto the wooden sticks, taking care to vary shapes and colors.

Depending on how much time you have and how many people you'll be serving, arrange the threaded fruit on a medium or large serving platter. Another way of serving it is to use one of the melons as a base and secure the bottom of the sticks in the melon so that they stick out of the melon.

If serving a large group of people, a watermelon is always a show piece. (I recently served one at a baby shower and it was a big hit!) Cut in half and serrate the rim so it looks like the teeth you cut in a pumpkin at Halloween. This is a nice accompaniment whether you're serving several sweets or appetizers. You could also use a wide-mouthed glass vase. Be creative! People who are watching their weight are always grateful for low-calorie options. Shows you're a caring host or hostess. Enjoy!

Amazing Ebooks & Paperbacks for FREE

Go to www.dianneharman.com/freepaperback.html and get your FREE copies of Dianne's books and Dianne's favorite recipes immediately by signing up for her newsletter.

Once you've signed up for her newsletter you're eligible to win autographed paperbacks. One lucky winner is picked every week. Hurry before the offer ends.

ABOUT THE AUTHOR

Dianne lives in Huntington Beach, California, with her husband, Tom, a former California State Senator, and her boxer dog, Kelly. Her passions are cooking, reading, and dogs, so whenever she has a little free time, you can either find her in the kitchen, playing with Kelly in the back yard, or curled up with the latest book she's reading.

Her award winning books include:

Cedar Bay Cozy Mystery Series
Kelly's Koffee Shop, Murder at Jade Cove, White Cloud Retreat, Marriage and Murder, Murder in the Pearl District, Murder in Calico Gold, Murder at the Cooking School, Murder in Cuba, Trouble at the Kennel

Liz Lucas Cozy Mystery Series
Murder in Cottage #6, Murder & Brandy Boy, The Death Card, Murder at The Bed & Breakfast, The Blue Butterfly

High Desert Cozy Mystery Series
Murder & The Monkey Band, Murder & The Secret Cave, Murdered by Country Music

Midwest Cozy Mystery Series
Murdered by Words

Coyote Series
Blue Coyote Motel, Coyote in Provence, Cornered Coyote

Website: www.dianneharman.com
Blog: www.dianneharman.com/blog
Email: dianne@dianneharman.com

Newsletter
If you would like to be notified of her latest releases please go to www.dianneharman.com and sign up for her newsletter.

Made in the USA
Monee, IL
09 November 2021